T H E

P I G   I S   F A T

THE
PIG IS FAT

by

Lawrance M. Maynard

WILDSIDE PRESS

For
My Friends
who saw me through

PART ONE

I

A SARDONIC portent in the life of little Benny Wagner was the fact that he swallowed his first taste of whisky on the very eve of National Prohibition—the night of June the thirtieth, nineteen-nineteen. Millions of patriotic American citizens tried to drink the nation dry that night. Benny had decided that he would help them, that he would get gloriously drunk—"cockeyed" as he expressed it—for once in his life. He wouldn't do it because he liked the booze, for he didn't care for anything stronger than beer or wine, but there was no harm in getting cockeyed once in your life—especially when it could never happen again as long as you lived in the United States. Besides—and this argument carried great weight with the eighteen-year-old Benny—everybody was doing it.

Benny knew that he wouldn't be able to drink much while he was with Lou Warren. He would have to wait until he had taken her home. Lou, all soft loveliness in a new summer frock of white silk, her dark hair falling over her shoulders in the Mary Pickford curls she affected, warned him about that before she consented to let him take her out at all.

"We'll have to be careful, Benny. You know how

3

people are on a night like this. They'll probably be rough and a lot of them will be drunk, and I don't want you to get into any trouble."

"I guess not!" Benny agreed emphatically.

"You mustn't drink anything but a little beer. You won't, will you, Benny?"

Benny was a bit nettled. He wished that people would get over telling him what to do. Maybe some day he'd be his own boss. He always boiled inside when any one, even Lou, began to give orders. Well, Lou meant well. She loved him, he supposed, so she didn't mean to hurt him any by telling him what to do. Not like Ethel and his stepmother at home. They bossed him because they hated him. At least Ethel, his stepsister, did. 'The old lady,' Benny thought, 'bosses me around because she's afraid to hurt Ethel's feelings. Ethel got to be too much for her when she grew up. Well, Lou ain't like that.'

"Sure," he agreed with Lou, "I won't do no drinkin'. We'll just go down to Lido Beach an' mix with the crowds an' see the fun. We'll get a kick out of it, I guess."

That, thought Lou, was a good idea. They could dance a bit and maybe have something to eat, then walk out on the pier to see the celebration.

At Lido Beach they found a singing, shouting, frantically drinking and maudlinly drunken mob of men and women that surged along the huge amusement pier. Benny marveled that the country could have gone dry when so many people seemed so

4

anxious to drink. He did not know that he was witnessing the first abortive symptoms of the great contempt for the Amendment that was to reach its tragic crisis a dozen years later.

As they passed the Pirate Ship Café they heard the blare of the jazz band through the open windows, and they stopped a moment to listen. Suddenly a hand shot out from an open window, holding a small glass under Benny's nose. Benny looked up, startled, and saw that the hand belonged to a laughing young man with a paper hat on his head. He was one of a party at a table by the window, and he was offering a drink to Benny. In all of the cafés along the pier people were doing the same thing, passing out drinks to those who could not find room in the crowded cafés. There were thousands of revelers who were unable to find tables or standing room in the cafés and barrooms, and everybody was willing to help everybody else get drunk.

Benny took the proffered glass and lifted it to his lips.

"Don't drink it," said Lou.

"Why not?" Benny asked, a bit defiantly.

"You don't know that man. It may not be good."

"I guess it is," said Benny. "He's drinkin'. They serve good stuff at the Pirate Ship."

Benny swallowed the whisky and almost strangled. He quickly reached the glass through the window and dropped it on the table, then tried his best to keep from coughing. It was too much for him. He

5

had to stop and swallow a few times before he could get his breath.

"Gosh!" he exclaimed, "that—stuff—sure has—got a kick." He coughed again. Lou laughed.

"Serves you right," she said. Lou and Benny had reached the stage in their friendship when they could jibe at each other at times. They loved each other enough even to quarrel once in a while.

"I can't help it," Benny said.

"That's what you get for trying to drink whisky," Lou said.

Benny was humiliated. She was insinuating that he could not stand strong drink, and that was a slur on his manhood.

"It wasn't the whisky," he explained. "I just swallowed too quick and it went down the wrong way."

Lou thought it best to say no more. She could see that Benny was resenting her kidding, and she did not wish to spoil the evening.

"There certainly is a crowd out to-night," she said, changing the subject.

"Gee, Lou, it's funny, ain't it? Here they're celebratin' because booze is goin'—an' they're all drinkin' all they can. Wonder if they're really glad."

"They don't care," said Lou. "They just act this way because they need something to jump into."

"Jump into?"

"Well, that's the way it seems. Everybody wants

a thrill. They go wild every chance they get. Look how they did last November. Most of them never cared anything at all about the war until it was all over—then they went crazy. They hear all about what the boys over in France did, and I guess they feel a little out of things."

"Out of what things?"

"They missed the big thing over there. That's why the kids gave wild parties when things were closed during the flu epidemic, and that's why the old maids tried to go to war and drive ambulances. All those who stayed at home thought they were missing a big thrill."

Benny never had pretended to understand Lou Warren thoroughly. Sometimes she acted so old and talked like she knew everything in the world, and at other times she was like a kid. She was far over his head, and he sometimes felt that she looked right over him and couldn't see him. She read deep books, and she was always talking about her career. She wanted to be a great singer, and she seemed to have got the idea that because she wanted to be one she was one already. Just because she wanted to be something like that didn't make her so great, did it? Anybody could want to be a singer. Just wanting needn't make a person so superior. He was always afraid that she was talking down to him, high-hatting him. When she talked big like that it made him suspicious.

Where in hell had she got those funny ideas about

7

the mob of drinkers? Jump into things! Why couldn't she just say that the chumps were taking a last fling before the lid was slammed on? That was what he was going to do as soon as he got her home. Why hadn't he left her home in the first place? 'Hell,' he was thinking, 'if it wasn't for her I could mix up with this mob an' get cockeyed. She thinks that shot of whisky was too much for me, but, gosh, how good it felt after it got down. Sort of warm and tickly inside. Wish I had some more now. Didn't hurt me neither. Couldn't help choking on that first drink, but any guy might do that. Sure they would—ain't I seen guys choke on a glass of water? Just goes down wrong, thass all.'

Lou was a good kid, but she didn't understand men, and she didn't know about drinking. Everybody else was doing it, and here she was holding him back. 'Well, I can do as I damn please after I take her home. Good thing she's gotta be home by ten bells.' He'd have the remainder of the night to himself, to do with as he pleased. Saloons and cafés wouldn't be allowed to serve drinks after midnight, but that wouldn't make any difference. That wouldn't stop drinking. People who bought plenty before twelve o'clock could drink all night if they wanted to. There'd be plenty of music and dancing in the cabarets. All of them had advertised a big night. Lou wouldn't know what he did after he took her home. Serve her right, too, for trying to boss him that way.

8

He noticed that she was looking at him strangely, and he was a little sorry that he'd been thinking about her that way. No use acting irritated. It wasn't really her fault. Better talk nice to her.

"Guess there won't ever be another night like this," he said, watching her eyes and trying to impress his good-will on her. He never was sure of himself with her, never knew just what to say, how to treat her. He knew that he loved her, and that she loved him, but her superior knowledge was a barrier to full understanding. Sometimes he felt that it would help him if he could slap her face, bring her down to his level.

"It won't make any difference, will it?" Lou asked, her voice tinged with impatience. "What if there never is another such night? I should think you'd seen enough booze in your life."

Back of her mind, where her consciousness could not catch it, was the thought, 'I've got to hold onto him, make him all mine. I resent it when he approves of alien things, things that are not me.' Consciously she hadn't any intention to hurt him, but Benny thought, 'She wants to be mean. Tryin' to make a fool of me.' He flushed deeply and said:

"You goin' to start that again now?" He stopped suddenly and faced her belligerently.

"Don't stop here," Lou said anxiously, afraid of attracting attention. "You'll get stepped on in the rush."

"You don't need to talk to me like I was a baby,"

9

he said. "You know I'm a little older'n you anyway."

They walked on silently. 'I'm a man,' he thought.
'She can't make a fool outta me.'

Because he sensed that he really was weak he
found it galling to have to remind himself that he
was a man. He must assert himself, convince himself that he was strong and not to be ruled by a
woman. He would always be afraid of people, and
always be hurting himself trying to prove that he
was not afraid. He would always resist Lou simply
because by giving in to her he would seem weak, and
he was determined to resent such an implication even
from Lou.

Consciously, his mind was seeking something in
hers, something to follow, something to understand.
He was so bewildered, so beset by doubts and sus-
picions. Lou was trying to dominate him, a man.
'I'm a man—a man,' he thought, and then he said:

"I'm a man, you can't boss me. See?"

"Big man!" jeered Lou. Why was it that she was
always irritated when he tried to be independent?
She wanted him all for herself, and she wanted to
absorb him. 'If he resists me he'll drift away,' the
unknown mind warned. 'I can't let him think even
of himself.' She didn't know that she was afraid of
losing him, that she was terribly jealous and that
she resented every thought in his head. She knew
that she did not like to hear him expressing opinions
of anything, especially approving opinions, and that

she could not help jeering at him. And then, it was so ridiculous to think of him as a man—him with his baby-blue eyes and clear white skin, him with his five feet-two of height. A man—why, a man would have rights of men, rights denied to women. No, she wanted him as a child. She resented him as a man.

Benny was thinking of her slur on his father's business, and of her jibe at his size. He was self-consciously aware of his under-size, and Lou's open mention of it always hurt.

"My old man's saloon is just as good as your old man's barber shop," he defended, understanding perfectly the meaning of her reference to booze. "Anyway, my old man never gets cockeyed like yours does."

It was Lou's cue to become indignant. "He does *not*," she exclaimed vehemently, "and you know it."

"Well, I guess he does," said Benny. "You know he does. I bet he's cockeyed to-night."

"Benny Wagner, if you're going to insult me this way I'm going right home."

"You insulted my old man an' me first," Benny reasoned, "so I guess you ain't got any kick comin'."

This time it was Lou who stopped and took a chance of getting stepped on in the traffic.

"You can't talk to me that way," she said firmly.

"Well, I guess I got just as much right to talk as you have." To himself he thought, 'Hell, I wish I hadn't said anything. No use fightin' all the time. She thinks she's right about everything, an' there's no use talkin' to a woman like that. I guess she loves me all right, but she just knows too damn much. All she thinks about is her music, an' she gets the idea I'm dumb 'cause I don't know about music.' Again they walked along in silence, thinking bitterly.

Benny was afraid, in his bewildered, jealous way, that, talented as she was, Lou would go too far with her music—too far for him to hope to tag along. He wanted a girl who'd be *his*,—not one who'd belong to the public, one who'd keep him like she'd keep a stuffed doll or a poodle. He thought: 'She'll think she's too good for me. Well, she ain't. No girl is.' But he was only trying to convince himself that he had escaped the tyranny of women—the tyranny of Ethel. He could keep telling himself that he was as good as any girl, and maybe he could forget Ethel running him out of the house, and the silly little girls whispering about him openly and giggling—giggling at some secret humor they'd found in *him*. 'I'm a man,' he thought, which was merely a hastily conjured idea—not really a thought at all, but an invention, a counterfeit—to cover up the skulking whisper at the back of his mind: 'She's an educated girl, and I'm a fool. I'll never be anything but a fool. Ethel told me so. Mother thinks so too. People never will respect me or take me as anything but a joke. Women will laugh at me. I can't understand it at all. Other fellows are happy

with their girls. Why am I so different? Why—
why—why—'

But these thoughts never found expression in his
conscious mind. He didn't know that he felt inferior. He knew only that he didn't want Lou to
become a great singer, so great that she'd stop loving
him. He never really thought the words 'Why—
why—why—' that were in back of his bewilderment,
but he opened wide his blue eyes and looked crushed
and hurt when things went wrong.

And then Lou broke the silence, trying to justify
her own unreasoning attitude.

"A gentleman never contradicts a lady," she said.
Immediately she thought: 'I made a mess of that.
That's too bromidic. That's a platitude for morons.
He'll think I'm silly.' So she was more irritated,
and became angrily silent. And Benny said the thing
most calculated to make matters worse.

"How the hell is a gentleman goin' to know a
lady when he sees one?" he asked. "Women all look
alike." The only time Benny ever swore before
Lou was during one of their frequent spats, and
she seldom noticed it—probably because she saw
nothing wrong in mild swearing anyway. But now
she was torn between her desire for peace and her
pride.

"That isn't a bit funny," she said. Tears began
to burn at the backs of her eyes, and she wished that
Benny would give in and say he was sorry. Quarreling wasn't in the least what she wanted. She seemed

always to be quarreling with Benny and then wishing for him to make up. Maybe someday, after she'd had a little more experience, she wouldn't be quite so amateurish with men. In books the women who loved men always held pleasant conversations with them in the moonlight—and there was plenty of understanding and love to last clear on beyond the last chapter. If the women quarreled they did it politely—called it repartee. They always said their clever and biting things laughingly, and the men always retorted wittily, but not so wittily as the women. Somehow, whenever she quarreled with Benny she had to be crude about it, always winding up in tears at the end.

"I think," she said, "that I had better go home—right now."

"All right," agreed Benny. He was quite willing that it should be so, for then he would have more time to get gloriously cockeyed before the fatal stroke of midnight. "We'll catch the next car to the city. I'll take you home, then I'll come back."

She looked at him anxiously.

"Benny," she said, "what are you coming back for?"

"Well," said Benny, "it's early yet. You don't expect me to go to bed at half-past nine, do you? It's only nine now."

"I don't care when you go to bed," Lou asserted.

"Well, let's go then. We'll get you home quick as we can."

"Benny, you're not coming back?"

"Why, sure I'm comin' back, Lou. There won't ever be another night like this. I sure ain't gonna miss it."

For a moment Lou said nothing. There was nothing she could say that would adequately express her emotions. She was trying to change emotions into thoughts, so that she could say something that would convey her fear of what Benny was coming back for and at the same time sound sensible. It was strange that she should feel that way, but she had a premonition that all was not to be right with Benny. No reason at all, she told herself, for feeling that way. Benny had never been drunk in his life. The glass at the window of the Pirate Ship had been his very first taste of whisky, his very first taste of anything stronger than wine. After to-night there would be no more chance for him to drink. Why should she be afraid of something he had never had before, something that after to-night he could never have again?

The tiny glass of Scotch seemed not to have affected Benny very much after the coughing was over. She had permitted him two glasses of beer in a lunch room and had told him he'd had enough. She didn't want to be a kill-joy. She recognized the innoxious quality of a glass of beer, and had even shared one with him. But enough was enough. She didn't want Benny to come back to Lido Beach once he had taken her home. Any other night it would

15

have been all right, for a minor couldn't buy drinks anyway, but nobody paid any attention to age to-night.

"Please, Benny," she begged, forgetting her grievance now that her maternal feeling for him had been aroused, "promise me you won't get drunk to-night."

Benny laughed.

"Get drunk! Why, Lou, you know better'n that. I never been real drunk in my life. Don't want any more Scotch either. Not to-night. I like beer."

"You can get drunk on beer," said Lou, "if you drink a lot of it."

"I like wine, too," said Benny. "Nice sweet stuff, like Port."

"I know, it's all right," Lou admitted, "but I don't want you to get drunk."

"I put sugar in it," said Benny. "It's good that way. You can get cockeyed on it all right, but it makes you sick before you get that way. Does me, anyway. I don't see why. It goes great at a party. Every time we have a party we get a gallon. . . . Gee, we won't have it after to-night . . ."

They had turned and were walking back toward the entrance to the pier. On both sides were the blatant beach concessions, mechanical thrill-rides— the Big Dipper, the Bobs, the Gadabout, Over the Falls, the Old Mill, the Virginia Reel—all filled with screaming men and women who seemed too gay to be sane. There were the gaudy booths, where for ten cents you could take a chance at winning a kewpie doll or a box of candy. Hot-dog stands and lunch-rooms were wedged in between cabarets and restaurants, and in all of them were crowds of drinkers. A hash-house with three tables and a counter was crowded by people who had been unable to get into cafés, and who had brought along their own liquor. From somewhere had come a trio of black musicians—banjo, saxophone and violin—and their jazz, as they played such popular numbers as the new topical "Sahara—We'll Soon Be Dry Like You," had transformed the little place into a miniature night-club.

Benny and Lou stopped and watched the antics of the negro players, and Benny sighed.

"It's bigger'n New Year's Eve, bigger'n Armistice night—bigger'n any celebration the beach ever had," he said. Then he added, "And it's the last time it ever can happen. Gee, Lou, I'm kinda sorry."

"It'll be hard on some people," Lou agreed. "I guess a lot of men will lose their jobs and everything, but maybe it'll be for the best after all."

Benny started to speak, but just then the negroes struck up again, and one of them began to sing in a high tenor:

"Saharrrrrrra, we sympathize with you.
Saharrrrrrra, we'll soon be dry like you.
I know why Cleopatra placed that snake against her skin.
She lost her mind completely when she lost her Gordon
    Gin.
Omar Kháyyám
Took a leap into his car-ar-avan

17

Grabbed his jug of wine and then he flew.
And ever since those old Egyptians waved their funny
    arms so queer.
They got that way from reaching for imaginary steins of
    beer.
Saharrrrrrra, Saharrrrrrra, we'll soon be dry like you."

Some one in the lunch-room was lifting a glass of
gin and offering a toast, "Here's to crime and Prohibition." Benny was looking a bit serious as the
music stopped.

"My old man is losin' his business," he said.

"He can open another one," Lou reminded him.

"Yeah, I guess he can," Benny admitted. He
really hadn't given the matter much thought. He'd
thought of the saloon as a respectable business for
his father ever since he had been old enough to sit
up and take notice of anything, and even now he
could not imagine his father in any other business.
He had thought of Prohibition as something remote, something designed to curb the lawless, and
his father had never discussed the matter with him.
The old man had gone on selling drinks just as he
had sold them for thirty years, and as far as Benny
could see he had made no move whatever to meet
the end. No wonder, then, that Benny had failed
to realize that after to-night his father would no
longer be in business.

"Gee," he said thoughtfully, "I wonder what the
old man will do, anyway."

18

"Maybe he can run a soda fountain," suggested Lou. "The papers say that a lot of the saloons will be made over into restaurants and stores. There's always something to put in a building."

"Gee," said Benny, "ain't we got enough restaurants and stores already?"

"No," said Lou. "Now there'll be more money to spend in them. That's what the Prohibitionists say. They explain it all in the papers. You ought to read the papers, Benny."

"Well, I don't see how my old man is goin' to know anything about any business but saloons. Maybe he knows, though. He never said nothin' about it to me."

"He's got money."

"I guess so."

Both of them were a little uncertain about it.

II

AUGUST WAGNER'S saloon had peacefully flourished for thirty years, and even the most ardent foe of alcohol could not truthfully condemn it as a den of vice or a sink of iniquity—phrases peculiarly characteristic of the holy crusaders in their onslaughts against the windmills of sin. Conviviality had always been the keynote of Wagner's success, and his own beaming goodfellowship imbued his patrons with a spirit of mellow brotherhood that precluded any suggestion of sordidness in the atmosphere. Men did not become drunk and fall senseless on the floor of August Wagner's saloon. Little girls did not burst tearfully through the swinging doors to plead pitifully for dear father to hasten home ere poor ailing mother passed away of starvation. If anything like that ever had happened in August's saloon he would have impoverished his till to buy food and shelter for them.

August didn't deny that there were saloons where such things might very well occur, but he claimed scornfully that the poor drunkard was apt to be less at fault than was his wife at home. In the old days, before the sad passing away of his own mate, he had often said:

"Me and my wife, we love each other. Do you
think I would get drunk and beat her, or spend all
my money for whisky and let her starve? Hell, no!
Go take a look at the women who get starved by
drunk husbands. You'll see why the poor men
take to drink."

Truly, August loved his wife, honored her, treated
her with stolid tenderness. But this could not last.
Life comes and life must go, and something went
wrong with the big woman who had worked hard
with her hands all her life but was not strong enough
to give birth to a baby. August puzzled over this
for many days, and felt that somehow he had been
cheated. She had simply ceased to live when the
baby came.

At that time the saloon had been twelve years old.
Not yet had August become prosperous enough to
hire help sufficient to run the place without him
always on hand. How, then, could he take care of
a new-born boy who was learning to cry harder every
day? He had hired a nurse, a widow, a woman who
came recommended by the doctor. He would keep
the nurse a year or two, until the baby was old
enough to be left alone in the house, then he would
manage somehow. He named the child Benny, and
then proceeded to delegate its care to Angela Chester, the nurse. He told himself that as soon as little
Benny should reach an age of usefulness he should
be put to work in the saloon. No loafing son for
him. He'd had to work hard for all he'd got, and

Benny must do the same. He would teach the boy the trade from the bottom up, and some day the saloon would descend to him.

Too bad, though, not to have a mother for the child. Too bad Dora had to die like that, leaving them both alone. He admired the way Angela Chester took care of little Ethel, her fatherless daughter. Ethel without a father, Benny without a mother, and yet here were a father and mother living in the same house. The more August thought of the situation the more he liked the idea that was forming in his mind. And when he finally spoke to Angela Chester about it he found that the idea wasn't exactly new to her either. They were married a year after the death of Dora.

Time passed. August was quite satisfied with things. He was in the saloon from ten in the morning until after midnight, and he had no way of knowing what methods were being used in the rearing of Benny. He did notice that the baby was a bit puny, was not as active as he thought a growing baby boy should be. But Angela seemed satisfied. When he mentioned his doubts of his son's perfect health to her she stiffened a bit and frowned, then she snapped:

"Augie, you just don't know about children. They all look that way when they're kids like little Benny. He'll grow up all right, and you'll see how he fills out. He's a strong boy."

August did not press the point. He did not like

to oppose the opinions of Angela.   And she seemed
to have some quite decided opinions on some things.
Right after their marriage she had started to assert
herself.   She had demanded the best of everything
for her own child, Ethel.   The little girl was a
willful, pouting, overbearing child even then.   She
seemed to grow more and more indifferent to the
rights and comforts of others as she grew older.
When Ethel wanted bread and jam she got bread
and jam, and she got it instantly.   If it wasn't forthcoming she shouted and screamed until her mother
was distracted and begged her to be a good girl.
But in Angela's mind Ethel was always a good girl.
She never punished the child, never more than
mildly reprimanded her.   At times, when the child
was more than usually unruly, even more insolent
and arrogant than was her wont, Angela would look
at her rather hopelessly, with a pleading expression
in her eyes.   The little girl was bullying her mother,
and her mother was afraid to say or do anything.
But she was not afraid of the little Benny.   She was
not consciously cruel to him, but she thought her
only real duty was to her own child and so she
neglected August's baby while she lavished all her
attention on Ethel.   Benny was given skimmed milk
while pouting Ethel drank cream.   Poor little Benny
did not gain strength as fast as he grew, and his
bones seemed large because there was so little flesh
on them.

Ethel, five years older than Benny, hated her stepbrother jealously. When Angela, on very rare occasions, took the baby in her arms or treated it with any tenderness, the little girl stood off and watched silently, with her lips curled in a strange expression of loathing. She hated to see her mother wasting affection on the baby, even though she herself was cold to her mother's caresses and often turned her face when Angela tried to kiss her. While the boy was yet an infant in his crib she began to take delight in tormenting him. One day Angela had caught her pinching the baby's toes, grinning slyly, cruelly, as she heard his first cries of pain.

"Ethel, what are you doing?" Angela cried, shocked in spite of her blind love for her daughter.

"Jus' playin'," the six-year-old Ethel had replied. "I like to play with the baby."

"But, honey, you mustn't play like that. You make him cry."

Ethel had looked at her mother with a sort of withering contempt, much too old an expression for a child.

"I don't care," she said finally. "He cries funny."

Her mother looked at her in some amazement, then assumed the expression of hopeless pleading that was becoming more and more common to her when dealing with Ethel. She said no more. Ethel, coldly disregardful of her mother's feelings as well as those of Benny, had already begun to rule Angela.

When Benny was ten, the fifteen-year-old girl

24

knew how to humble him and torture him without
touching him. She had her girl chums, and she loved
to have them come to the house for luncheon and to
play girl-games in the yard. The girls, older than
Benny, would come, laughing and whispering among
themselves, and as they whispered in one another's
eager ears they would cast sly, tormenting glances
at Benny, and then they would giggle in that cruel,
vulgar way of the school-girl who is beginning to
learn the half-truths of the gutter. Benny never
knew what it was all about. He only knew that they
left him out of things, and that they made life very
miserable for him. He never could play in the
yard, or in the house, even for one day without
this attack by the forces of Ethel. And then came
Ethel's sixteenth birthday, and the gay party of boys
and girls of her own age. Benny looked longingly
at the cake and the freezer of ice-cream. It would
taste good, he thought, and on this one day there
would be boys as well as girls in the house. He
would not be an outcast. But Ethel decreed other-
wise. On the morning of the party day she said at
breakfast:

"You better go play with the boys somewhere to-
day, Benny. I'm giving a party, and you'll be in
the way."

"But ain't I goin' to be at the party?" Benny asked,
feeling that something had dropped from under
him.

Ethel laughed scornfully.

"I don't want you," she said bluntly. "You go off somewhere for the afternoon."

"Where'm I goin' to go?" he almost whimpered.

"Find some of the kids from school."

"Aw, most of the kids are away in the summertime. Anyway, I get tired of always havin' to go lookin' for them. Why can't I ever play at home . . . and why can't I—come to—your p-p-party?"

"You just can't," Ethel said unfeelingly, even smiling at his obviously tearful speech. "It's *my* party," she went on relentlessly. "It's my *birthday* party. You can't come."

Benny, who had not had a birthday party in all his eleven years, felt that he must be very unimportant in the world. He did so want to enjoy himself and to be loved, and it seemed that nobody even recognized his existence. Nobody, that is, but Ethel —and she just noticed him to chase him out of her way. Ethel, at sixteen, had a permanent pout, a perpetual expression of irritation mixed with boredom, and Benny always felt that she was getting ready to spring on him. And then, there was Mrs. Wagner always agreeing with everything Ethel said. Those two were always right, and Benny, it seemed, wasn't worth listening to or even slightly considering.

Why didn't his stepmother tell Ethel to let him be there for the party? Angela just sat placidly at

26

the table and ignored her daughter's cruelty. To her, mere words meant little. Had Ethel struck Benny, or thrown a plate at his head, she might have mildly remonstrated; but Ethel was merely striking the boy with words, and she saw nothing cruel in that. Besides, Ethel was speaking very pleasantly, and not at all quarrelsomely. She was very glad that her daughter was so refined. It showed gentle breeding, and Angela was beginning to find it necessary to grasp hopefully at any signs of gentleness in Ethel. She hoped, a bit wistfully, that her daughter loved her.

And so Ethel had her party, and Benny spent the afternoon wandering in the park. After that Ethel did not whisper about him among her girl friends. Whenever she had guests she deliberately told Benny to make himself scarce. It got so that nearly every afternoon Benny had to find company for himself or play alone in the streets or in the park. Ethel became more and more brutal in her dominance over him, and he became more and more humble in her presence. If he felt any resentment toward the arrogant girl he did not betray it in his speech or actions. Sometimes he just looked at her in a bewildered, thoughtful way for a moment, and then he would go off by himself and cry the hurt out of his heart. Benny cried a lot then, for he found that it strangely soothed him. He was trying to understand something of his life, but it seemed that it was a thing not to be understood easily.

27

It seemed that there were so many things in the world that were hard to understand. In school his teachers sometimes smacked his hands with a ruler or humiliated him before the entire class by calling him a dunce. More than once he had been stood up in a corner, his tearful face to the wall, the laughter of the children ringing in his ears. School-children can be more cruel than any adult simply because they do not know what it is to intend to be cruel. With his face to the wall, standing in the corner, he would try to keep the tears back. They would come anyway, and this would hurt him more than the punishment. Sometimes as he stood there he would think of rebellion, and picture to himself the consternation of the room should he suddenly turn on the teacher and tell her to go to hell. What if he should slap her? Would they stop laughing at him then? Or would they defend her and beat him for her?

Then there were the long days when he was made to stay after school because he had not known the exact answer to a question which the teacher had seemed to think very important. Teachers were always asking questions, some of them very silly questions that were easy to answer, but some of them questions that seemed impossible to answer, impossible to *have* any answer. He could never, for instance, remember the date of something called the Magna Charta, or who it was who did something on a hill in Darien, or what war was called the War of the Roses, or who said something very important in Revolutionary times, or what states were the origi-

28

nal states. Teachers were always being horrified when he couldn't tell them these things, and he was forever wondering why they should get so excited about it. A fellow would think a teacher would get so tired of all that stuff that she wouldn't care what answers you gave her. He always looked surprised and bewildered when he was told to stay after school and write something a thousand times. He didn't exactly hate school, for Benny had been brought up with the understanding that he had no right to hate anything, since he was so very insignificant himself, but he was suspicious of it and could see no use in it. He discovered that some of the bolder spirits of the school played hookey, and the first time he slipped off to a park instead of going to school he felt an exhilarating sense of freedom and strength. He began to mingle with the rougher element among the boys, and to find his escape from home frustrations in escapades with the gang.

One of the first things he learned, then, was that Chick McTeague, the tough son of Alderman Mc-Teague, was to be recognized as the leader, the "big shot," of the gang. From him the boys learned much of the ways of the world. Chick was older than any of the others, and his knowledge of evil was beyond his age. He always had a girl, and in a supercilious, man-of-the-world way he instructed the younger boys in the first principles of sex and its biology. Chick was arrogantly conscious of his father's position, and the boys looked up to him and considered him an admirable object for emulation.

29

III

A FAVORITE loafing place for the boys was in Ed Warren's barber shop, two blocks from August Wagner's saloon. Ed's business was not very large, and he did not mind the company of the boys, who used his shop as a club room. He liked to listen to their boasting talk of escapades and conquests. He was unimaginative, and their highly colored tales left him wondering and puzzled. His was a matter-of-fact mind, and the prosaic trade of barbering had offered few opportunities to enlarge his horizon. He heard the boys talking of love and its adventures, and he blinked stupidly at their revelations.

"You kids don't know a damn thing about it," he would say.

Ed Warren was forty years old, and he didn't see anything very thrilling in love. His wife was just like any other woman, wasn't she? Sure she was, and they couldn't make him think they were getting anything he'd missed. He'd been married nineteen years, and he ought to know all about it by this time. Ed Warren was primitive. He ate when he was hungry, drank when he was thirsty, rested when he was tired, slept when he was sleepy—and when he

wanted a woman he took his wife. What more was
there to enjoy in life? Of course, he had to work
too. He had to earn money to be able to have all
the other things. Maybe some day something would
happen to make him rich; then he wouldn't have to
work any more. He could spend his time just eating
and drinking and resting and sleeping. Maybe he
could let his daughter Lou study music like she
wanted to. Lou had funny ideas, but he guessed it
was all right. Lots of girls were singers, and he understood some of the good ones, like this here
Geraldine Farrar, who'd just got a good job in the
movies, got a thousand dollars a week for it.

Of course, Lou would never make big money like
that, but maybe if she got good enough she could get
a job in a cabaret. People did say that Lou had a
swell voice, all right. He liked it himself when she
sang "Smiles" and "Till We Meet Again." She had
something sad in her voice when she sang "I'm Always Chasing Rainbows" or "Dear Old Pal of
Mine." But, hell, she'd have to learn to sing the
jazzy stuff if she wanted to make money at it. Well,
she was a good kid even if she was so high-falutin.
He'd sent her to high school, and that was something to be proud of. Damned right it was. Lou
knew a few things.

The boys used to like to talk to Lou when she
came into the shop to bring her father's lunch at
noon. Ed Warren never went home to lunch. He
always said that he might lose a good customer if

he wasn't in his shop all day. So Mrs. Warren would fix up a nice lunch and Lou would carry it down to the shop in a basket, the hot dishes wrapped protectingly in napkins. Sometimes Lou would bring along some extra food and they'd eat together. Lou was quiet, and the boys respected her instinctively. She didn't exactly snub them, but her natural refinement was like a protecting armor about her. When they talked to her they did so shyly, half afraid of their own tongues. Benny worshiped her at a distance for a long time. When he finally did speak to her he found himself sinking into the depths of her beauty. Lou sensed something, and the feeling that came over her was a thing for which her education had not prepared her. She began to single him out of the mob when she found the boys in the store, and when he spoke to her she looked quietly into his eyes and forgot for a while to be superior.

Lou had nothing to fear from the other boys. Even Chick McTeague respected her. Her intelligence placed her on a plane to which he could not aspire, and he did not resent it. She was not his kind of girl, and he scorned those who were not his kind. A girl had to be a "good sport" to win the favor of Chick. And so, although Chick was the leader of the gang and had always been given first choice of anything the gang acquired, he did not interfere when Benny began to win the friendship of Lou Warren. The rest of the gang looked on with cynical amusement. If Benny Wagner wanted to be a chump and fall for a flat tire like that, why, let him do it. The girl would make a chump of him.

It was in Ed Warren's barber shop that the first really criminal job to be carried out by the gang was planned. Strangely enough, Lou Warren was the inspiration of it. In the neighborhood lived a wealthy old woman who was known to all as the Widow. It was not known just where she had got her money from, or just when her husband had passed on, but everybody agreed that she was a widow and that she had more gold than she could count.

One day while the boys were in the shop the Widow passed, and Lou, smiling a bit wistfully at Benny, said:

"If I had a little of her money I could go to Europe and become a great singer."

"Has she got much?" asked Benny.

"Yes, they say she's got millions."

Chick McTeague's ears were quick to catch the sound of money. He left the rest of the boys in the corner of the shop where they had been talking confidentially and came over to the window-seat where Lou and Benny now habitually isolated themselves from the mob.

"She ain't got so much dough, has she really?" he asked.

Benny spoke up, anxious to verify anything that had been said by Lou.

33

"Sure," he said, "the Widow's a regular old miser. Keeps thousands of dollars in her old house. Never spends nothin' either. Must have a million bucks salted away. Don't keep it in no bank, neither."

The other boys, seeing Chick interested, had become all attention themselves. A million dollars! What a treasure to work on the imagination. The seed was planted. Almost without talking about it the gang decided that the Widow's hoard must be raided. It was known that she went for a walk every afternoon at two o'clock. She lived alone, without servants or relatives. The house would be deserted. Chick McTeague, as the leader, was elected to ransack the house while the rest of the boys watched the neighborhood to see that he was not disturbed.

Chick did get into the Widow's house. He stayed there an hour, and when he finally emerged he had a yellow cat under his arm. The gang followed him back to Ed Warren's shop, where the loot was to be divided. Lou was sitting in the window-seat. Chick walked over to her and tossed the cat in her lap.

"Here, you can have it," he said.

Benny went over to Lou and stroked the cat, while from half a dozen throats came the question:

"Where's the money?"

"There wasn't no money," Chick said.

The boys were stupefied. They all looked strangely at Chick. One of them said:

"What the hell did you take the cat for?"

34

"Well," he said, "the damned thing kept purrin' around all the time. I couldn't find no dough, an' that made me sore. So I just grabbed the cat an' beat it outta there. I just took the lousy cat 'cause I was sore. What about it, hunh?"

They had dreamed of a million dollars, and they had got a yellow cat. They did not upbraid Chick, nor tease him about the cat. His attitude toward his action was one of arrogance, so that the whole episode took on an air of heroism to the boys. Chick had a way of assuming that everything he did was absolutely right. Who were they to doubt it.

Lou touched Benny's arm and whispered:

"Benny, I don't like Chick. You'd better not be too friendly with him."

Benny was astonished. "Why, Lou," he said, "Chick is a regular guy. His old man is an alderman. He's a big shot."

"Are you always going to let the big shots step on you?" Lou asked cryptically.

"Aw, Lou, you don't understand. Chick's a good guy."

"Yes," said Lou, "I know. He's a big shot."

Benny looked at her, wondering just what was behind that innocent remark. He stroked the cat again, and his hand brushed hers on the cat's back.

"He gave you a cat anyway," Benny said.

"Yes," Lou agreed. "He gave me a cat. I suppose his father gives your father things too. They're big shots."

35

"It's a good cat," Benny insisted.

"It's a very good cat," Lou said. "A big shot gave it to me. What use has a pig for a cat?"

She was beyond Benny. He continued to stroke the cat, and his fingers continued to touch hers until finally their two hands rested together on the back of the cat.

Next day one of the fellows came into the shop when Chick and the other boys were there.

"I seen Mike Kennedy, the harness bull, down the street," he said. "Somebody stole the Widow's cat, he says. Says the Widow is drivin' him crazy 'bout 'at fool cat. Says she thinks she's gonna die 'fore night if she don't find her cat. He says she loves 'at fool cat 'cause it's the only livin' thing 'at ever could live in the same house wit' her."

"Well, what of it?" Chick demanded.

"Well, you don't want Mike Kennedy to be driv crazy by 'at old Widow, do you?"

"Who the hell cares?"

"Well, you don't want 'at old Widow to go off an' die 'fore night, do you?"

"Who the hell cares?"

Chick's indifference added much to the gang's awe of him. Here was a man defying the law and the Widow, not to mention public opinion, all in the same breath. In the eyes of the gang, the stealing of the cat took on the proportions of a vast crime. Vicariously the boys were covered with glory. Were they not permitted to share in the exploits of the great Chick McTeague?   Benny looked up to his idol with augmented respected, and wondered if he could ever become as fearless and independent as was the son of the alderman.   These were bold thoughts for the Benny who had been driven from his own house time after time by a stepsister.   These were the thoughts of the new Benny, the emerging Benny, the Benny in revolt—although his revolt wasn't understood by him in the least.

Somewhat to the disappointment of the boys, Mike Kennedy didn't quite go crazy, nor did the Widow die before night.   Eventually the yellow cat found its own way home, and everything was thus adjusted. Only Lou seemed a bit grieved.   She had grown fond of the cat.   She remembered how Benny's hand had found hers on the sleek yellow back of the cat.

The boys went back to their games of stealing apples and potatoes from the vegetable wagons, after which they would roast the potatoes over a fire in a vacant lot.   Only Chick McTeague had any idea of what his goal was to be.   He was planning while the boys were playing.

Benny himself never considered as criminal, or even as mildly wrong, the stealing of fruit from the Chinese vegetable venders, or the filching of sweets from the candy jars in a grocery store.   It was all a part of the game, all play.   Because he had never been allowed to play at home when Ethel wanted the house and yard for her own games, he entered into his new-found freedom with abandon,

37

and joyfully took his share in all the escapades of the gang.

When Lou Warren definitely took her place in his scheme of things Benny began to neglect the gang. He took Lou to the movies, and she taught him to dance. Holding her tantalizingly close in a fox-trot, Benny felt a new sensation. The first time he kissed her she offered no objection, but the second time he tried it she repulsed him. He could not understand her then, and probably because she puzzled him as everything else had puzzled him, he felt awkward with her at first. She knew so much more than he knew. She had been to high school, while he had only gone to the seventh grade and had made that only because he had cheated. She was even studying music, and only very intelligent people could do that. She was always trying to explain to him how music was born in a person, and it didn't take great intelligence to love a thing that you were born to love. When she said that Benny was inspired to say:

"I was born to love you, I guess."

As soon as he said it he blushed and would have left her in confusion if she had not grasped his hand and told him she was glad.

They were so young, and they were trying to be so old. They wanted to act like experienced adults about their love, but even Lou with all her education and talent had not been to the school of Cupid yet. She was really afraid of being in love, for she had

38

seen something of what it could do at home and she
was not sure that she wanted to go through with it.
But Benny was sweet, and she wanted to cuddle him
and know that he was hers. Perhaps some day they
would marry—someday after she had won fame as
a great soprano. Lou had known since she was ten
years old that her destiny lay in music.

Her big brown eyes widened and sparkled with
the wonder of it when she pictured for Benny the
brilliant future that was to be hers. Benny caught
some of her enthusiasm, but at the same time he
felt the old bewilderment. Surely he could not hope
to have this great singer for himself. If she went on
to fame she would leave him behind. In his eyes she
read the hurt that he did not express in words, and
she very clumsily tried to comfort him:

"I love you, Benny. You know I do. But I've
got to be sensible about it. I can't let anything interfere with my music."

Benny had looked so hurt then that she had taken
his hand and said softly, "We'll be happy, I know we
will."

In her mind she was saying: 'I wish he could understand. I do love him, but I won't let him take
my mind off my voice. I've got to study and make
something of myself. Love will have to wait. If
he won't wait I'll have to forget him.' When she
realized what that meant she caught herself desperately. 'I can't lose him . . . I can't.' But she
sensed the impossibility of her situation. Benny

would never understand. She could never teach him to appreciate music as she loved it.

When Benny was eighteen he had to register for the draft. The war was beginning to demand the boys now that the men had gone. August spoke to his wife about it one night, but she replied, "Oh, Benny won't be taken. He's underweight." August looked at his son, and was a bit startled to notice how small he was for his eighteen years. Perhaps he would have tried to do something about it, but suddenly he was confronted by a new worry. Prohibition was coming, and he was to lose his business.

Sometime during the thirty years August had got a permit and had installed a little distillery of his own in the large warehouse back of the saloon. For years he had been making a brand of whisky which his patrons claimed was as good as most of the high-priced bottled goods. The warehouse was well stocked with whisky and other liquors, and old August wondered what would happen to his distillery and his stock. What was the intention of the Government toward such things? Would there be some legal use for the vast supply of liquors? Old August questioned every one of importance who came into his place, but nobody seemed to know the least thing about it. None even pretended to know until one night Alderman McTeague waddled into the saloon and laughed ponderously at August's bewilderment.

"Don't worry about nothin'," he said, his thick lips drooping so that his mouth seemed to arch upward from the corners of his chin, "everything'll be taken care of all right."

August didn't particularly care for McTeague, but the fat politician was the boss of the ward, and as a saloon keeper and wielder of some few votes in the district August found it necessary to tolerate the man who controlled his local destiny. Just as long as August supported McTeague and his henchmen at election time the ward heeler would protect August in the matter of licenses and permits, which seemed to be required every time the saloon keeper moved a spittoon or added a new brand of beer to his stock. McTeague was tall, with the heavy, awkward build and carriage of a giant bear. He was never known to stand still, for he was forever swaying back and forth from one foot to the other when he was not sitting or walking. When he talked he had a habit of taking short steps back and forth in front of his listener, and these steps were a series of swayings and waddlings. He would shift his weight to one foot, then move the other a few inches and shift his weight to it. People who talked to him on the street usually left him gladly, for he had an annoying way of making one nervous.

Although McTeague was tall, heaviness was the one impression left on the minds of those who saw him. He was never called big, for his weight and height seemed divorced somehow from bigness. His face was heavy and oily, and he wore glasses with heavy gold rims. His hair was thin on top, and he

wore a heavy derby hat to cover it. At municipal
affairs and ward dances he wore a gleaming silk hat,
and his dignity expanded accordingly.

Probably McTeague had done little real harm to
any one in the district. Grafting shamelessly from
the city, he protected his own district in certain things
that had to do with taxes and improvements, and
asked nothing from the district but faithfulness at
elections. That some voters considered faithfulness
to be best demonstrated by double voting or mayhem
on other voters was no concern of McTeague's. He
didn't tell them to do it, and he didn't pay them
to do it. If he handed out any cash it was because he
thought the receiver needy. He once offered to
prove this in court when a nosey newspaper accused
him of buying votes. His classic assertion at that
time had been:

"Why the hell should I buy votes? I ain't runnin' for no office."

He got away with it, because most of the people
really couldn't see why a man who wasn't running
for anything should buy votes.

Except for the formal affairs when he wore his
silk hat McTeague was very careless of his appearance. His clothing hung loosely on his awkward
body, and he never bothered either to have his suits
cleaned and pressed or to buy new ones. On his
ring finger he wore a diamond that had cost two
thousand dollars. He smoked dollar cigars, but
when he was hungry at noon he always drank a glass

of beer and filled up on free lunch in August Wagner's saloon—and he never paid for the beer.

McTeague waved a pudgy, moist hand in a gesture of scorn for August's worry. He blinked his gleaming little pig-eyes under his projecting brows and laughed.

"Everything it goin' to be taken care of," he said. "You won't lose anything. Just sit tight and act wise, and you'll see."

Well, if Alderman McTeague was so sure about it everything had to come out right. He'd just take the politician's advice and wait for events. August had great faith in politicians. He had seen what they could do.

August thought it funny that the Government should order Wartime Prohibition after the Armistice had been signed and the war was all over, but he supposed maybe the Government knew what it was about. The country would go wet again as soon as the A.E.F. was demobilized. Then he could keep his saloon open until the final dryness should come in 1920. Maybe he wouldn't have to close at all. Maybe demobilization would be accomplished before Wartime Prohibition was to take effect the first of July. But he waited in vain. People began to say that the nation was going dry for all time on the first of July, and that maybe it would be years before the army was demobilized. The Eighteenth Amendment would take effect while the wartime act was still in force.

43

August never did get the matter completely clear in his mind. He didn't read the papers very closely, and he found nobody who seemed to know just what it was all about. He knew only that people said he'd have no business after the last day of June. But what of McTeague? August was greatly confused.

By the first of June August was resigned to the impending new order of things. McTeague's assurance came back to his mind. Something, no doubt, would be done at the last minute. After all, he wasn't alone in his loss. Others would be trying to do something. Thousands of saloon men all over the country would be forced out and thousands of their employees would go out with them. It was certain that something would be done about it.

Thinking that the saloon might not close after all, August put Benny to work as a porter's helper. Benny was glad of the independence derived from a small income of his own. He seemed to thrive on the work, and was always fresh and smiling. Small and supple, he seemed to have an inexhaustible supply of energy that kept him tirelessly at work during the three hours he was in the saloon each forenoon. He polished the brass and mahogany of the bar until it shone with the unsullied luster of virtue. With unceasing industry he rubbed the huge mirrors back of the bar until they were as clear as crystal and their reflections took on an air of reality that sometimes caused slightly tipsy patrons to imagine that they were looking from behind the bar into

44

the saloon instead of from before the bar into the
mirrors. Everything in August Wagner's saloon was
as spotless and shiny as was the rounded bald pate of
August himself. Benny's task was to keep it so.

This was a good start for Benny, thought August.
Of course, the Alderman might be wrong and everything might be lost, but it wouldn't hurt to start
training Benny. If things didn't turn out right, why,
Benny had profited by the work anyway, hadn't he?
He hoped McTeague knew, though. Anyway, it
wouldn't help matters any to worry. Probably
things would adjust themselves somehow. He
wouldn't starve. He had a little money put away
—enough to last him the few years he had left to go.
Perhaps he'd even have enough to give Benny a start
in life. If not, then Benny would have to make the
best of it by himself. On the morning of the last
day of June he opened his saloon in the cheerful
manner of a man who has decided to make a new
start in life, and who is enthusiastically interested in
the new adventure. He joked with Benny, and
Benny thought that his father must be very happy
about something.

"Here's a new cake of Bartender's Friend," August told him. "Make the old place shine like a
new shoe, Benny. All our friends will be in to-
night."

"I'm goin' to the beach to-night," Benny said.

"To the beach?"

"Lido Beach. Special celebration to-night. Callin' it 'Last Chance Night.' I'm takin' Lou."

"All right, then. Lou is a good girl. I'm glad she's going with you."

By noon Benny had finished his work, and he left his father busily directing the cook in the kitchen, for old August had made preparations for a last-night free lunch that would be long remembered by his friends and patrons.

The crowd began to arrive early that night. By seven o'clock the saloon was crowded. Three deep the men stood at the mahogany bar, and August lamented the fact that to-night he could not keep the bar polished and spotless as it had been through the years. This wasn't the peaceful group of convivial men who had gathered there as his patrons and friends so many times in the past. This wasn't a beer-drinking, story-telling, ballad-singing crowd of good fellows enjoying a night of recreation. This crowd that had come to greet the Eighteenth Amendment was a hard-drinking, profane mob of grim hedonists, determined to get drunk at all costs. There was a new kind of fraternalism manifesting itself for the first time in America. It was the fellowship of defiance and scorn of the law. Men bought bottles of whisky and passed them through the crowd. Everybody drank frantically, and nobody cared who paid for his drinks or whose drinks he paid for. Bartenders rang up all the money that was tossed on the bar, and gave no change except

46

for large bills. They served drinks and did not com-
plain if no payment was forthcoming. It was a
night of reckless drinking, and of the reckless serv-
ing of drinks. And old August Wagner was shocked
when he saw that for the first time in his life women
were drinking in his saloon.

Promptly at midnight he closed his bar and began
trying to clear out the remaining patrons. His three
bartenders had tossed aside their aprons, going off
duty for the first time without bothering to clear
the bar. August didn't know what to do with the
fourteen men he found soddenly asleep on the floor.
He couldn't make them stir, and nothing like that
had ever before happened to him. He didn't want
to call the police. His saloon was respectable, and
to call the police would disgrace it. He looked at
his bar and saw broken glasses and pools of liquor
all over the mahogany that had once been immacu-
late. His bartenders collected their last wages and
went home. August stood in the middle of the floor
and surveyed the ruins. He looked at the fourteen
men, and a sob filled his throat. Lush-bums passing
out on his floor—in his nice clean saloon . . . in his
respectable place of business . . . after thirty
years. . . .

Respectable? Good God, why think of that now?
A man could work hard all his life, and then this
would happen. Damn Prohibition and all the reformers . . . Was this what they had wanted to
bring about? Why worry about calling the cops

47

now? Why try to keep up at all? The law had closed his saloon, and had brought a bunch of drunks to pass out on his floor. By God, he'd make the law clean them up. Let the law carry out its own refuse. . . .

"Listen, Mike," he said to the patrolman on the beat a minute later, "there's a bunch of drunks passed out in my place. Call the wagon an' run 'em in. I'll stick around and close up when you're through."

"How many of 'em?" asked the cop.

"Fourteen," August told him.

"Fourteen! Say, August, you don't want me to run all them guys in do you? It's a big job."

"What the hell do I care?" thundered August. "You're hired to do it. The country's dry now, an' it's against the law to be drunk. Call the wagon."

Half an hour later, as he locked the door of his old saloon, he thought: 'No business now . . . Still got the building. . . . Got to pay taxes just the same. . . . Got to start a new business. . . . Damn it, I'm too old. . . . Don't know any other business. . . . Guess I can do it, though, if I have to. . . . Maybe open a restaurant . . . Use the bar for a lunch-counter . . .'

He went on home, and when he got there he was surprised that Benny had not yet come in.

.   .   .   .

Benny took Lou home, and as he told her good-night on the front steps of her flat she took his hand in hers and said:

"Benny, please don't go back to the beach."

"I want to," said Benny. "I'll meet some of the fellows down there, an' we'll just have a little fun foolin' around in the crowd."

"Benny, please don't get drunk."

"You know I won't, Lou."

"I'm afraid."

"Why?"

"Benny—you know why. If you start drinking you won't be the same. I don't want you to change."

"Don't be silly, Lou. Nobody can drink after to-night anyway, so why worry?"

"But they will Benny—they will drink."

"How? Ain't the country goin' dry to-morrow?"

"Oh, Benny, why can't you do as I ask you to just this once? I won't sleep if I know you're at the beach."

"Why?" Benny was strangely affected. He had never seen Lou so intense. It made him want to give in to her. He looked at her quizzically, and said again, "Why?"

"You know I love you, Benny. I don't want you to get away from me."

Suddenly she was crying, and Benny had her in his arms, telling her that he would stay away from the beach and never do anything to hurt her. She stroked his hair, and he felt the tears in his own eyes as she told him how foolish she knew she had been to act that way.

"You know I'll always love you," she said.

He looked so small as they sat on the front steps, he on a step below her with his head against her breast and his wheat-straw hair tickling her bare neck, that she wanted to mother him and protect him. She felt that she should always be his protector, that he would always be as a child to her. Not yet had she begun to think of him as a lover.

He turned his face up to her lips and she kissed him, and then she had to jump up from the steps and hurry into the house because from somewhere upstairs they heard the voice of Mrs. Warren calling querulously.

Benny, as he left Lou's house, was thinking: 'She's sure a good kid all right. Means a lot to me. I won't go back to the beach. I'll find a good movie and take it in. Forget about booze and Prohibition. Keep my promise to Lou. . . .'

But before he found a good movie he was found by Chick McTeague, the burly son of the fat alderman. Chick had developed grandly, until he was the envied of all the sheiks who were forced to admire his sartorial perfection. He always had plenty of money, and he sported a new Stutz roadster in which he roared about town. As Benny walked down Sixth Street he heard the open muffler of Chick's car, and a second later the strident voice of Chick was hailing him.

"Climb in, Benny," the big shot invited.

"Where you goin', Chick?"

"Down to Lido."

"Been there already to-night," said Benny. "Thanks just same."

"Aw, come on. Hot time down there to-night. You'll meet some right guys."

"Not to-night."

" 'Fraid o' your girl, eh?"

Chick knew that Lou Warren had taken Benny from the gang, and he never missed a chance to jeer at Benny's softness. Now, as he smiled with those crooked, twisted lips of his, Benny knew that Chick was thinking him a sissy and a chump. Benny still looked up to Chick. Chick's old man was a big shot in the district, and Chick could pretty near have anything he wanted. Chick's old man could even tell Benny's old man what to do. Here was the son of the big shot kidding him—thinking he was afraid of a girl. Well—he wouldn't let Chick think anything like that.

"All right," he said, "I guess I might's well go along."

Chick McTeague grinned approvingly as Benny seated himself in the car and they started in the direction of the beach.

"Atta boy," he cried, "you stick with me an' you'll get along O.K."

IV

THE right guys to whom Chick McTeague had promised Benny he should have an introduction had reserved a booth at the Ocean Inn. There were two of them, young sheiks who wore derby hats and talked from the corners of their mouths to prove they were tough. They were Chick's type exactly. The underworld called them punks, but they thought they were big shots. They greeted the newcomers noisily, and with an immediate proffer of drinks. Then they remembered themselves and looked at Benny suspiciously, with their eyes narrowed to slits. This proved that they were dangerous men to play with. They had learned it from the movies and the newspapers. Chick saw what he thought was in their minds, and he laughed.

"This is a pal o' mine," he said. "Benny Wagner. His old man runs a saloon in my old man's ward. Guess you know what that means." He pointed to the tallest of the two youths, and said to Benny, "This here is Spike Davis."

Spike Davis had a flat nose and thick lips. His eyes had a strained look, and that made his whole face look like he was ready to cry. He shook hands with Benny and said:

"Pleased ta meetcha."

"Sure he is," said Chick. "This other guy is Eddie Sheehan. He's a good guy."

"Glad to know ya," said Benny, shaking hands with Eddie Sheehan. Eddie was tall, and had a thin, cynical face. He wore a pearl pin in his tie, and he was always fingering it when he talked. He took Benny's hand with his right hand, and touched the pearl pin with his left-hand fingers. Benny looked at the pin but didn't say anything. The pin didn't look like much. Eddie smiled at Benny and said:

"Sure, it's a good pin all right. I wear a guard on the end of it under me tie."

Benny didn't care, but he told Eddie he thought that a very good idea.

"Yeah," said Eddie, "some cannon might like the looks of it."

"What's a cannon?" Benny asked.

"Hunh!" Eddie exclaimed, "the kid don't know what is a cannon."

"He's green all right," said Spike.

Benny was sorry he had asked. He didn't like to be laughed at—especially before Chick. But Chick spoke up for him.

"You guys ain't so wise," he said to the two gangsters. "I bet Benny knows a lot o' things youse guys never heard of."

"Yeah—maybe," said Eddie.

"A cannon's a dip," Chick said to Benny.

53

"Sure," said Benny, "I know."

"He knows," said Eddie. "Yeah, sure, he knows."

Benny felt out of things. These guys were friends of Chick's, and Chick was all right, so of course he ought to like them. Chick was his idol, and Chick's friends came recommended, but had he met them under unbiased circumstances he instinctively would have avoided them. They did not radiate friendliness. They sneered, and acted too superior for him. Of course, Chick acted that way—but Chick had a right to act that way; Chick was a big shot. Well, the fact that Eddie and Spike were so superior just proved how good Chick was. Even with these two big guys he was the leader.

The table was laden with bottles and glasses, and more had been ordered as soon as Benny and Chick arrived. The others drank easily, and Benny tried to toss off the whisky and gin with the sang-froid of the old timers. It choked him, but he stuck bravely to it, and grew dizzy after the third drink. Chick looked at him and grinned.

"Lap it up, kid," he said. "There's plenty more where that come from."

"All right," said Benny. "All right, Chick, I guess I'll get rid of my share."

Eddie looked at him and frowned.

"Say," he said, "what about your share, hunh?"

"I guess I can drink all right," said Benny. He didn't like to seem weak before Chick's friends.

"T'hell with what you can drink," Eddie growled. "What about your share of the bill?"

"That's all right," said Benny, somewhat taken aback. "I got some money."

"Sure, he's got money," said Chick.

"He'd better have," Spike put in.

"I got enough," Benny said. He had thought he was their guest, and now they were demanding that he pay, but that was all right. He wasn't a cheap skate. Eddie relaxed and said:

"Well, I guess you know this ain't no charity performance. Cover charge to-night is ten buck apiece to begin with. You pay for what you drink, too."

Benny looked suddenly wilted. He signaled frantically to Chick and whispered:

"Gee, Chick, I didn't know what it was goin' to be. I only got eight bucks with me."

Chick opened his eyes in astonishment.

"Only *eight bucks?* Say—what the hell do you think you're pullin'? What'd you come for?"

"I didn't know where you was goin'," Benny stammered, really frightened now.

"Well, you oughtta know where you're goin' when you go places. You oughtta know it costs dough to play around with this mob. What you gonna do about it now?"

"I don't know," said Benny. "I only got eight bucks."

"What's the matter with him?" demanded Spike. "Think we're a bunch o' chumps?"

"Eight bucks, hunh?" said Eddie. "That ain't so good. Better come across, kid."

"I haven't got it," Benny almost whispered. He looked from one to the other, half hoping to find sympathy in one of the sneering faces. Eddie and Spike were looking at him silently, their eyes half closed, their faces holding the expressions they thought should be on the faces of desperate and dangerous men. Suddenly Chick broke the silence, snapping his fingers and smiling.

"Benny is O.K.," he said. "He didn't know we was goin' to spend dough. He can get it to-morrow. I know his old man. Let him drink all he wants. He's good for it."

Benny was relieved, and very grateful to Chick. Chick was his friend. He was standing good for his drinks. He'd sure pay Chick to-morrow. Good old Chick. A real pal. Gee, it was great to have a friend like that. Do anything for Chick now. Chick was all right.

Since childhood Benny had looked up to Chick as a being stronger and mightier than himself, but there had been nothing personal in his admiration. He never had considered Chick as a friend, but rather as a great person who was to be emulated as closely as possible if one would be a big shot. To him the alderman's son had been as a general to his trooper, but now the officer had condescended to befriend the helpless private. The life of the private, therefore, should be at the command of the general.

56

Benny would devote himself to his friend Chick McTeague. He was seeing Chick now through the glasses of whisky and gin he had taken, and Chick looked very good to him.

The gangsters settled back in their chairs and laughed.

"We had the kid scared all right," said Eddie.

"Yeah, he thought his time had come. Wonder what he thought we was goin' to do to him anyway."

Benny had not thought of what they might do to him. It had seemed to him that he was in danger, and that was enough. When two burly gangsters sit in a café booth and glare at a man who had offended them, that man does not think about what they can do to him; he thinks about how he is going to placate them or get away from them. Now that they were all smiling and friendly again, Benny was at ease and felt a bit sheepish.

"I'll pay Chick all right," he said.

"Sure you will," said Chick, winking at the others. He filled Benny's glass and Benny swallowed the whisky—this time without coughing. "You shouldn't never be busted," Chick continued. "You oughtta have plenty dough."

"Old man's been payin' me ten bucks a week," Benny explained.

"Ten a week! Why, that ain't cigarette money."

"Oughtta be settin' purty," agreed Spike. "Old man runnin' a s'loon an' all."

"Saloon closes to-night," said Benny.

"Your old man's got a lot o' booze stored away, ain't he?"

"Yeah, he's got some all right."

"Well—" began Eddie, but Chick silenced him quickly.

"Dummy up," he snapped.

Eddie looked resentful, but he subsided. Chick gave Benny another drink. Benny's head began to feel heavy. He nodded sleepily. Chick smiled and winked at Eddie. Suddenly Benny jerked his head up and stared strangely at Chick. He pushed his chair back and got unsteadily to his feet.

"I'm goin' home," he said.

"Sit down," said Chick. "What's eatin' you now?"

"I'm goin' home."

"Have another drink," said Chick. "You don't wanna go home."

"Sure I wanna go home," said Benny. "I gotta go home."

"Stick around," said Chick. "Maybe I'll show you how to make some money."

"Aw right," Benny said. "I guess—I guess—I wanna—make—s'money aw right."

"Sure you do. Everybody wants to make some money. There's lots o' dough to be made, too."

"Aw right," said Benny.

"You jus' wait a while an' keep yer trap shut, an' I'll have you wearin' diamonds."

"Aw right."

58

"An' don't go shootin' off your mouth to that broad you're sweet on. Women is dangerous animals. All right for a good time, but no good to get tied to."

"I gotta go home," said Benny. "An' say—whatcha mean anyway—hunh? Whatcha mean? Lou— Lou's all right, she is. Damn right she is—all right —with me. I guess I gotta go home."

"You're a damn fool," Chick sneered.

"No'm not. I'm sick . . . I don' feel ver' good. I wanna go home."

"Aw, hell," said Eddie, "the kid's stewed to the gills. Don't know what it's all about."

As if to verify the gangster's diagnosis Benny suddenly slouched forward and let his head rest on the edge of the table. He was trying to think, but something was wrong with his head. He knew he should have gone home. Shouldn't be here with Chick at all. Chick had insisted. Well, he couldn't get in wrong doing what Chick wanted him to do. All of his life Benny would be a follower of the big shots, letting them use him, imagining that he was one of them.

He could hear the buzz of voices and the clash of a jazz-band, but they seemed far away and remote from his being—like a scene that is distortedly and dimly perceived through a heavy fog. When he tried to raise his head and look about him he saw that the lights apparently had dimmed, and the faces of the men at the table had grown grotesquely

small and unreal. Everything seemed to float in dim
space before his bewildered eyes, and he dropped his
head back to the table with a sigh. No use trying to
figure things out when they looked like that.

He heard distant laughter, and was dimly aware
that it had come from Chick McTeague. What was
Chick laughing at? He'd like to know what the
joke was, so he could laugh too—but he couldn't lift
his head to say anything. Seemed like something
was holding him down, like it sometimes does in a
nightmare. Distant, floating voices were drooling
strangely, mingling laughter and curses with jazz
music and singing and the clink of glasses. Somebody was saying:

"He's passed out all right."

"Yeah; he can't stand it yet. Just a kid. He's
got a good head though."

"An' his old man's got hooch."

"Plenty."

Floating words, drifting over him and into his
ears but meaning nothing at all to him. He was like
a drowning man who feels the water pressing down
on him, and hears the beat of the waves just before
he slides into unconsciousness. He was filled with
thoughts, all jumbled and incoherent, like funny
pictures in his mind. Rushing out of them suddenly
came Lou Warren, smiling and laughing and point-
ing a finger at him like a mother who is teasing her
naughty infant. He lifted his head and cried out:

"Lou—you tol'—me not to—drink—you know—

how many drinks I had—af'er you tol' me that—
Plenty—yeah, plen'y. . . ."

"He's got the D.T.'s," said Chick, grabbing him
by one arm and holding him in his chair. Eddie and
Spike were both drunk, but they didn't stagger or
pass out. They just sat straight in their chairs and
looked at Benny.

"We gotta get him out," said Chick.

They carried Benny out and placed him in Chick's
car. Benny knew nothing of it. He was unconscious
of the ride back to the city, and did not know that
his father helped Chick put him to bed. Benny was
experiencing his first drunk, and he was not aware of
anything that was going on. When old August
Wagner went back to his own bed after seeing that
Benny was safe he found that his wife was awake.
She had heard everything.

"Drunk, was he?" she snapped. "Nice way for
a boy like him to come home. He'll come to no
good end, I'll bet."

"He won't do it again," August assured her.

"He's *your* son," she mocked. "Your son—
startin' out to be a drunkard. Drinkin' in saloons."

"He never drank none in *my* saloon," August suddenly almost shouted. "No kid ever got anything in
my place. Prohibition made Benny drink to-night.
It's the damned law."

"August! August! Don't yell so. The neigh-
bors will hear you yet. You don't dare say things
against the law. It's part of the Government."

61

"The Government, hunh? Yeah, sure, the Government. For thirty years I pay taxes to the Government. For thirty years I buy licenses and pay out my money to the Government. What does the Government do now? Yeah, what does it do? It closes me outta my business and makes my little son drunk so he can't see. To hell with such a Government."

"Don't talk like that, August." Mrs. Wagner was frightened. The war had made free expression of opinions unsafe.

"Well, it makes me mad. I try so long, then I lose everything. I think I'll do something. I think maybe people won't do what the law says all the time."

During the rest of the night August tossed on the bed, awake and thinking of what the law had done to him.

PART TWO

O LD August didn't do anything about his saloon until after the middle of January, when the Eighteenth Amendment finally took effect and intoxicating liquor was defined as anything containing more than one-half of one percent of alcohol. When August heard that he laughed and said he'd like to see the man who could get drunk on a barrel of even four percent beer.

The Government bonded August's warehouse and stationed an armed guard there to see that none of the booze got away. It seemed that the powers that be had decided that physicians still could prescribe whisky for sick people, and so the bonded whisky in August's warehouse was to be taken out a little at a time by special Government permit. He wasn't to have anything to say about it at all. The Government was even making saloon keepers and brewers pay storage for the privilege of keeping their stock in bonded warehouses belonging to the Government.

Old August gradually absorbed all the facts, and he became more and more bitter against the law that had taken away his business, the business that had always seemed decent and respectable to him. He read a speech by an Anti-Saloon League man who said that the saloon had always been an outcast from decent society, and that no decent, right-thinking citizen had ever approved of it. This made old August very indignant, and he cried out that because a few saloons had been dens of vice this man was ignorantly condemning them all. Whenever the preachers wanted to condemn a thing they picked out the very worst example of that thing they could find and then proclaimed that it was typical of all, and that anybody who would uphold such a thing was a soulless degenerate. What about the churches themselves? he demanded. If you wanted to knock the church you could pick out a meeting of Holy Rollers or maybe go to Zion City and pick out the crazy lunatic that said the world was flat, and then you could say the whole Christian religion was rotten because some people who didn't know any better were acting like nuts and calling themselves Christians. What would the preachers say if you did that? Well . . .

Old August was trying to get his bearings in his new world, and he may have been a bit incoherent. He had no idea of what was to come, and he didn't like the idea of running a lunch-room. He and Benny had begun the work of remodeling the saloon right after the Amendment took effect. They enlarged the kitchen, and arranged tables in front of the bar. Benny suggested a soda fountain back of the bar, and for a moment old August looked at him half belligerently. Then he sighed and said:

66

"All right, Benny—we'll have a soda fountain. We'll sell ice cream and soft drinks."

An expression of gentle sadness crept over his face as he looked at the mirrors and brass work back of the bar. He looked at the gleaming beer-spigots and shook his head.

"We don't have to take 'em out," he said. "We can use 'em for something else."

"Sure," said Benny brightly, "near-beer'll come through 'em just as easy as the regular stuff did."

"Sure, near-beer. . . . I guess even Anheuser Busch makes it now, hunh?"

"They all make it," said Benny, "an' they got some stuff they call Bevo. It tastes like beer, I guess."

"Maybe it does," said August doubtfully. "Maybe it does."

And so the spigots that once had gushed forth the mellow, amber liquid with the white collar of lively, feathery froth, the liquid that trickled so easily and soothingly down hot throats in the summertime, the liquid that went so pleasantly with a lunch of cold meats and cheese or with a hot meal of corned beef and cabbage, became the spigots from which issued a sluggish stream of a flat concoction called near-beer. It wasn't long until people began to spike the near-beer with alcohol, and it made them sick and sometimes it even made them drunk—which was a thing the old real beer had never done.

Benny and Lou continued to see each other,

67

though she was practicing her music more than ever now, and was talking of going to work so she could save for a trip to New York where she could take singing lessons from a famous teacher. She hadn't said much about Benny's dereliction on "Last Chance Night" at the beach. Of course, she'd heard of it. There had been much talk in Ed Warren's shop, and although Benny had long since ceased to meet Lou there—for they no longer wanted to meet in the presence of the gang—it did not take her long to learn the truth. When she spoke to him about it he admitted it readily, a bit ashamed but still a bit defiant, as though to let her know that while he thought a lot of her no woman had the right to make a sissy of a man.

"Didn't you love me enough to keep your word to me, Benny?" she had chided.

"Sure, Lou, you know I do. But I guess you just don't understand those things. I'm a man, Lou."

"I'm afraid you are," she replied, and left him to puzzle over that.

II

AUGUST'S interest in running the new restaurant was desultory. He found that people who ordered glasses of near-beer were disappointed; they expected the real thing, and it hurt him to see them wink suggestively when they said "near-beer." It hurt him more to have to give them literally what they asked for.

The man who guarded the warehouse during the day became friendly. He would come into the restaurant and order coffee several times a day. August suspected that the man was up to something, for he seemed to expect August to spring something. He was always hinting, and seemed to be hanging around waiting for August to say something. August was puzzled. He had no idea what it was the man wanted.

Another thing he didn't like was the way Chick McTeague hung around Benny. Chick could not mean good to anybody but himself. He would come into the restaurant and sit in a booth eating his lunch and talking to Benny. It wasn't pleasant to see his son becoming confidential with the alderman's son. The older McTeague might be all right. He was a politician, and he had sense enough to keep clear of trouble, but Chick was just a thoughtless tough, depending on his father's power to keep him out of jams. Sometime Chick would try something that would land him in jail, and he wouldn't care how many of his associates he took with him. The sad thing about it would be that Alderman McTeague would get his son out of it, but the others wouldn't have a drag and they'd suffer.

"What's Chick McTeague talk to you about?" August asked Benny one day.

"Nothin' much," said Benny. "Why?" Benny was annoyed at his father's curiosity.

"I just don't want you to get mixed up with him," August warned.

"Don't worry," said Benny. "Chick knows what's what all right. He ain't dumb. Anyway, he ain't up to nothin'. Just likes to eat here 'cause he knows me."

But that noon Benny sat in a booth with Chick, and Chick lowered his voice almost to a whisper while he told Benny of his plans.

"It'll be a good start for us, anyway," he said. "Won't be any big money in it at first, but we can branch out when we get the customers."

"We only got about a hundred gallons," Benny said.

"That's all right for a start. We can sell it for seven bucks a quart."

Chick took an envelope from his pocket and asked

70

Benny for a pencil. With a thoughtful frown he labored at the figures. When he had covered the back of the envelope he tossed it to Benny triumphantly.

"Not so bad, hunh," he said, smirking with satisfaction. "One hundred gallons at seven slugs a quart is twenty-eight hundred bucks—almost three grand."

"It's good money," Benny agreed.

"An' it's dead easy," Chick assured him. "The stuff's in the basement of your house. All you gotta do is pack it out an' we'll sell it."

"How we gonna sell it?" Benny asked.

"Hell, you ain't dumb are you? It'll be easy to sell. Why, old Fat Hall down at Lido Beach is sellin' it in coffee cups over his lunch counter—an' he's gettin' four bits a shot for it."

"You said seven bucks a quart," Benny reminded him.

"Well, if you sell it by the drink you can make more. Anyway, you can cut it with water."

"Yeah," said Benny, "I guess we can do that all right now."

"Gosh, Benny, that's a new one. Funny I never thought of it."

"What's that?"

"We figured a hundred gallons your old man stored in his basement. Well, we can make a hundred an' twenty-five gallons outta that easy. That'll give us—le's see—" He began to figure on the face

71

of the envelope. The result elated him. He smacked his hand on the table.

"Three an' a half grand!" he exclaimed.

Benny began to wax enthusiastic now.

"An' if we sold it by the shot—that'd be more, hunh?"

Chick thought a moment.

"I guess you can get twenty drinks outta a quart," he decided.

"That'd be ten bucks a quart 'stead o' seven," Benny said.

"You sure?" Chick used the pencil again and nodded. "Yeah, that's right," he agreed. "You guessed good that time."

"I didn't guess," said Benny.

"No? Well, le's see how much a hundred gallons'll bring us at ten bucks a quart."

"We figured a hundred an' twenty-five gallons," Benny reminded him.

"Yeah, that's right. We're gonna use water, ain't we?" He got busy with the pencil again, tearing open the envelope to use the blank inside of the paper.

"Jees!" he exclaimed suddenly, "that'd be five grand! Five grand! We're gettin' in the money, kid."

"But, hell, Chick, if we sell it by the shot we won't get all that dough at once. It'll come in slow."

"Sure," said Chick, "but if we keep on we'll be makin' plenty later, I guess."

"I guess so," Benny agreed.

"Maybe later on we can sell it in big lots, an' make some big dough."

"Yeah, but where we gonna get it?"

"We'll find it all right," Chick promised.

"I don't see how."

"Your old man's got a warehouse full, ain't he?"

"Aw, that belongs to the Government now. They got some stuff from other saloons there too. The old man says there's a million gallons there. But we can't get any of it. There's a guard there all the time."

"Well, just wait. We'll find a way. There's other places got booze."

"What good's that to us?"

"Maybe a lot o' good."

"You mean we'll steal it, hunh?"

"I don't mean nothin'," said Chick. "What we gotta do is get that stuff outta your basement. We can sell some to old Fat Hall at Lido, an' I got a guy to take the rest of it. He ain't got no dough, but he'll sell it in his joint an' we'll split."

"Well, I guess that's all right," said Benny.

"Course it's all right."

"Sure it is."

Benny felt a bit important now that Chick Mc-Teague was taking him into his confidence. He began to feel himself a potential big shot, to class himself as one of the underworld. It was a bit thrilling to realize that he was in the underworld. That

73

was a word used in newspaper stories of robberies and murders and other mysterious doings. It was a word used in dime novels and what the boys called "shoot-'em-up stories." The underworld!—Why, it wasn't a place at all! It was just what you did and not where you lived. One day you lived honestly in a respectable neighborhood, and then the next day you were planning to become a criminal, and that made you part of the underworld without moving out of your respectable neighborhood at all. Since Chick McTeague had first broached the subject of bootlegging Benny had been trying to orient himself to the mythical underworld. While it frightened him a bit, he rather liked the idea. One thing, he could talk with the big shots now, and he could feel like somebody. Even Ethel couldn't bluff him any more. Some day he'd tell her to go to hell. Of course, it was against the law to sell booze now, but what of it? He'd started out honestly enough, but Prohibition had put his old man out of business. Might as well get as much as possible out of Prohibition, hadn't he? Sure.

"Who's the other guy you got to take the stuff?" he asked Chick.

"It's Ed Warren," Chick said.

"Gee—Lou's old man!" Benny blinked in astonishment.

"Is he gonna sell it really?"

"Sure; why not?"

74

"I guess it's all right. I just never thought it would be him, that's all."

"He's dumb," said Chick, "but he likes to make money. A dumb guy can sometimes get by. Nobody suspects him."

"Well, when're we gonna take the stuff over?"

"When can you get it outta the basement?"

"Any time, Chick. Ethel an' the old lady go out to Westlake Park every afternoon. The old man's busy."

"We'll take it this afternoon," Chick decided.

"All right—but how?"

"I'll drive the Stutz over an' you drag the booze out an' pack it in the back. It'll hold twenty gallons easy. That's all Ed wants."

"What about the rest?"

"We'll get it outta your house an' hide it at Ed's till to-night. Then we'll take fifty gallons down to Fat Hall at Lido. He'll take the fifty an' pay cash."

"How much?"

"I guess we'll have to let him have it for six bucks a quart. We ain't got time to fix it up like we said before. We made a mistake too; we figured retail prices, an' Fat Hall buys wholesale."

"That'll be twelve hundred bucks," Benny calculated. "That ain't so bad—six hundred apiece."

"Listen, Benny, you gotta remember that Spike Davis an' Eddie Sheehan are in on this racket. We gotta split with 'em, too. We only get three C's apiece."

75

"What they gonna do?" Benny asked, a bit un-certainly.

"They're part of the mob," Chick explained. "They'll drive behind in another car to cover us to-night. Fifty gallons is a lot, an' we gotta carry part of it in front with us. Somebody might see it, an' we gotta be safe."

"Gee, only three hundred bucks? But what about this booze? Ain't I gettin' it all?"

"Listen, Benny, you ain't smart yet. You gotta have teamwork. You can't peddle the stuff alone, can you? Hell, you'd be in the can right away. If you wanta make dough you gotta put out dough— you gotta split your take. You gotta figure all that in this racket. Anyway, this is just a start. After while we'll be sittin' purty. We'll be makin' big dough, an' you'll see we'll need Spike an' Eddie more'n ever. I guess maybe we'll prob'ly have to take on couple o' more guys besides—later on. We gotta work together, an' we gotta split even with the mob."

"All right," Benny agreed. "I guess you know, Chick. I didn't mean to crab. Just wanted to know was all." Benny smiled reassuringly at Chick. Not for the world would he have the alderman's son think he was kicking. Why, what if Chick should refuse to have anything to do with him? He'd be out of everything just when he was beginning to get in good. "I don't know much about these things," he said humbly.

"Sure," Chick said affably, "you got lots to learn yet." He rose and stretched himself languidly, then shook his heavy shoulders. Before he left he turned back to Benny and winked.

"Take it easy," he said. "I'll be at your dump at two o'clock."

III

ALDERMAN McTEAGUE waddled into August Wagner's restaurant and eased himself into one of the booths, where he flopped down into the seat and pressed his fat finger against the call-bell button. August's one waiter, a ratty little Canadian named Louie McKay, hastened to the booth and pulled the curtain across the entrance. He looked at McTeague meaningly and grinned.

"Tell Wagner to come here," the alderman ordered. "Don't stand there and grin at me either."

"All right, boss. Everything's jake. Thanks for easin' me into this berth."

"All right; don't talk about it. Go get Wagner."

Louie departed in quest of his employer. McTeague waited, impatiently puffing at a Perfecto. When Wagner finally pulled the curtain aside and looked in, McTeague snorted and spilled ashes on the table. He pressed his finger to the call-bell button and motioned August to come in and be seated.

"When that waiter, Louie, comes tell him to bring gin."

"You're joking, Mister McTeague. But that's all right. Maybe you'd like some Bevo?"

"No," said McTeague, "I don't crave Bevo. Tell him to bring gin."

"You mean it?"

"Sure I mean it."

"But you know I ain't got it."

"I mean it anyway. Tell him to bring it."

August saw that McTeague meant it, but he couldn't understand. When Louie appeared August looked at McTeague, then he ordered gin. He said it with a deprecating smile, so that the waiter would think he was joking. He didn't want Louie to think him strange. But Louie's face remained impassive and he vanished without a word. In a moment he was back with water-glasses containing an inch of colorless liquor that looked like water. August's nose told him that it was indeed gin—of a very poor brand. He looked at Louie in astonishment, but McTeague laughed and told the waiter to be gone.

"You see," he said to August, "how easy it is. Louie is a friend of mine."

"Friend of yours?" August was trying to understand.

"Sure. I got him the job. Remember he came to you with a letter from me?"

"Yes, I remember."

"Well, I wanted my friends here."

"What's it mean?"

"Remember I told you not to worry about losing anything when Prohibition come in? Well, you ain't

goin' to lose anything. Ever notice the guards at
the warehouse?"

"Sure; they eat here."

"Sure they do. I told 'em to."

"*You* told 'em to?"

"Why not? They're workin' for me. I fixed
them up with their nice Government jobs."

"I see." August was beginning to get a glimmer
of the truth.

"They're all greased. All you got to do now is
hand over a little dough. The booze will be brought
in here. You can sell some here, but we got bigger
things lined up. Louie already knows his part.
He'll see to getting the stuff out of the warehouse.
The guards will help him. We'll all make money.
You can turn this joint into a speakeasy. I'll take
care of you. We'll go fifty-fifty."

"I can't do that," August objected. "It's against
the law, and I never did anything like that."

"You will now," stated McTeague.

"No, I think I better not."

"You can't turn me down. I got too much in it.
Anyway, there's no danger. I can protect you and
all the others. I can keep out competition, too."

"I can't do it," August objected.

"You will do it. You got to."

"I got to think of my wife and kid," August explained. "I can't take chances. I'm too old. I
might lose everything."

"Ain't I told you I'll make it safe for you? You

trust me, don't you?   Damn right you do.   You'll do it, won't you?"

"No."

"Listen, I'll tell you what we can do.   You can stay out of it, just like I am.   We'll run the business in somebody else's name.   You just sit back and take in the dough.   You own the place, but you lease it to a dummy.   You work here as his manager.   Just an employee.   No danger."

"I don't think I better do it."

A hard glitter possessed the eyes of the alderman as he thrust his face forward across the table and snarled:

"You want to stay in business, don't you?"

"Of course."

"Well, I guess you know I can run you out if I want to.   You know I can, don't you?"

"I run an honest business."

"I can prove you're a bootlegger.   Your waiter served gin to me right here, and you ordered it.   If the joint was raided they'd find gin and whisky. Now do you know I could run you out?"

"I guess you could."   August was looking at the alderman dumbfounded.   He had not known that the man was so utterly base.

"You *guess* I could!   Well, I *know* I could.   I know more'n you do—I know I *could* and I know I *will*."

Now that the man had shown his fangs, now that his mask of friendliness had been dropped to expose the true face of greed and corruption, August felt that he was better than the politician—that he no longer needed to dissemble. Might as well let the alderman know for all time how he stood. He looked quizzically at McTeague and almost whispered:

"That settles it then, hunh?"

"Sure that settles it. You're wise. We'll make plenty."

"But I ain't goin' to do it."

"*What!*"

"I'll hang onto what I've got instead of taking such a chance to get more."

"Think you got to obey the law, hunh?"

"Maybe."

"The law that put you out of business. Fine, ain't it?"

"Can't be helped, I guess."

"Plenty of wise business men are goin' to help it. You better get in with the first."

"I've never been a crook."

McTeague laughed. "Maybe you're tryin' to call *me* a crook, hunh? Well, for five million dollars I can afford to be called a crook. At wholesale prices there's five million dollars' worth of liquor in that warehouse. We can get it all. Crook! You better be a crook then, unless you want to starve. I'll run you out or put you in jail. What do you say?"

"I got to get back out front," August said quietly. "The rush starts about this time."

"You won't play ball?"

"No," said August, "I won't."

The deciding factor had been McTeague's threats. August revolted at the suggestion of force. Much as he hated Prohibition he hated blackmail more. McTeague had used the wrong tactics. Had he worked on August's dislike of the Amendment instead of on his fear of persecution he might have won his point. As it was he defeated his own purpose. Instead of causing August to assert his independence of Prohibition he had aroused an assertion of independence of McTeague.

"Well," said McTeague as he left the restaurant, "maybe you'll change your mind. I'll see you tomorrow."

"I won't change my mind," August called after him. A minute later he called Louie and told him he was fired. Louie merely laughed and said:

"All right, old man. I'll be back soon though."

August stood behind the cash-register and looked crushed. He began to wonder how much he could get for his business if he sold it. Maybe he'd better retire. He was getting old. As a matter of fact he was only fifty-five, but he felt a hundred.

'Guess I'd better sell out,' he thought, and he sighed as he remembered the thirty-one years he'd spent in this one place.

IV

FAT HALL weighed three hundred and fifty pounds. The fat on his gross, sweaty body lay in unhealthy folds that shook like jelly when he moved, making his breasts look like the breasts of a woman. When he talked he seemed always to be out of breath—like a runner who has just finished a grueling race; he wheezed and puffed asthmatically. When eating he grunted like a hog, gasping for breath between hurried mouthfuls. Snatching the food up as though he feared it would be taken from him, he would bend his head toward the plate and shovel it into his cavernous mouth with knife and fork. He would wash it down occasionally with huge swallows of beer, letting it run over the edges of his mouth and trickle down over his chin. He looked and sounded exactly like a pig at the trough.

Fastidious people who went into Hall's lunch-room to eat for the first time never returned. His repulsive animalism robbed them of all appetite for the really good food he served. His place at Lido Beach was patronized regularly by cheap pugs and carnival men and the riff-raff of the underworld. They appreciated his complete lack of moral sense and his inhuman brutality. They knew his past, and they respected him.

In the old days Hall had run a den on the Barbary Coast in old 'Frisco. He had been a king of the tenderloin, but finally he had been forced out because of a killing. He had been responsible for more than one killing in his joint, but this time he had happened to make a victim of the wrong man. Hall had dug into the man's skull with a sharp meat cleaver, a weapon he always kept at hand. The victim's head had been split like a block of wood that has been split by a woodcutter. Hall had to leave town when things got hot for him. He went to Mexico. For a while he smuggled yellow men across the border at five hundred dollars a head, but the Chinese head of the syndicate had grown tired of Hall's method of slaughtering valuable merchandise when he became enraged. Hall had found it necessary to leave Mexico or die. He chose to live.

He became a moonshiner in the mountains of Northern California before Prohibition. He made a particularly vile brand of rot-gut and sold it cheap to the lumber-jacks and other mountain workers who weren't too exacting about the quality of their booze as long as it had a kick. Hall's moonshine certainly had power if nothing else to recommend it.

Growing weary of the mountains, and motivated a bit by the fact that a number of husky woodsmen had suddenly passed away after drinking copiously of his wares, the moonshiner packed up his stock of rot-gut and moved to Lido Beach. He didn't sell any of his booze, for city people, he found, would not drink poison when they could get good stuff in

the saloons. He simply stored the stuff away until
Prohibition closed the saloons and opened a market
for him. The day after Prohibition took effect he
began selling his stuff in coffee cups at fifty cents a
drink. Also, he made up his mind to watch his
chance, and to go into bootlegging on a big scale as
soon as the opportunity offered itself. He'd not be
a cheap operator of a blind-pig either; he'd be a
wholesaler and sell the stuff for big money.

It was eight o'clock in the evening when Benny
and Chick entered the lunch-room and drew Hall
aside to whisper that they had fifty gallons of good
whisky near by. They had brought a small bottle
with them, and Hall tasted it and found it good.
This, he realized, was the sort of stuff that would
bring him good customers. It was the sort of stuff
that would help him on in the direction of the big
money and the power he craved. He would get the
money, he thought, and then he would boss the town.
People would have to toady to him then, not daring
to snub him or try to drive him out of town.

"Where you got it?" he asked.

"I got my car parked a block from here," Chick
replied. "It's all in the car. I can drive up the
alley back o' your joint an' unload."

"Bring it around," said Hall, his eyes gleaming in
excitement. "Bring it around and unload."

"It'll cost you twelve hundred bucks," Chick told
him.

"Six bucks a quart," Benny amplified, but Chick

cast on him such a withering look that he detached
himself in confusion, becoming a mere onlooker in
appearance. Inwardly he was feeling the old puz-
zlement and frustration he had experienced at the
hands of Ethel at home. But Hall was objecting,
saying the price was too high. He had to make a
hundred percent profit or he wouldn't buy.

"But if your stuff's all like what I tasted I'll give
you one grand for it," he wheezed decisively.

"Six slugs a quart ain't too much," Chick insisted.
"Give us twelve hundred an' it's all yours."

"One grand," repeated Hall, a note of finality in
his voice.

Chick looked at him a moment, half angry, half
wavering. The twelve hundred demanded was much
less than he and Benny had first figured, and here he
was about to lose part of that. Hall was trying to
jew him down, and Hall had a reputation for getting
what he wanted at his own price. He would probably have to take what the fat bootlegger wanted to
give him in the end, but damned if he'd give up right
away. No use losing any chances.

"Twelve hundred," he repeated.

Fat Hall got up and went behind his counter, a
sarcastically polite smirk on his drooling lips.

"Anything I can do for you fellows?" he asked,
elaborately ignoring Chick's last demand. "I got
some good spare-ribs an' kraut to-night if you like
'em. Look over the card an' see what listens good
to you."

Chick saw that it was no use. Benny said nothing. Hell, Chick knew his stuff. He'd come out all right. The fat slob couldn't get away with this stuff. Let Chick do the talking. Chick knew how to handle guys like this Fat Hall. He'd make Fat come across.

"Whatcha gonna have?" asked Hall.

"Aw, Fat, don't be that way," Chick begged. "You know we don't want nothin' to eat. Why don't you give us the twelve hundred, hunh? Ain't I been right with you?"

"The pot roast with spaghetti is up-to-date to-night."

"Aw, lay off that oil."

"The Hungarian Goulash with noodles is the real McCoy."

"Aw, hell then," Chick exploded resentfully. "Give us the grand then. You're a damn chisler."

"Now you're talkin'," Hall wheezed, nodding his head heavily. "Drive the stuff around an' unload."

Chick and Benny went back for the roadster. Eddie Sheehan and Spike Davis were half a block away, parked at the curb in a rakish little Ford that was called a speedster by the company that rented it to them. When they saw Chick and Benny they whistled. Chick went back and cursed them.

"You wanna bring the bulls down on us? Can that noise!"

"Aw, we just wanted to let you know we're here."

"I don't give a damn about you bein' here. Don't

make any more noise. The fat slob only wants to give us a grand."

"Well," said Eddie, "are you gonna take it?"

"Got to," Chick said. "The kid'll just be outta luck, that's all."

"Oh, yeah?"

"Yeah; we'll split nine hundred three ways an' give him a C."

"Right. That'll be three yards apiece for the three of us."

Chick went back to the Stutz and told Benny to hop in. In two minutes they were in the alley back of Fat Hall's lunch-room, and Hall was helping them unload the fifty gallons of whisky. They stored it all in the back room, behind a pile of boxed canned goods. When it was all stored Hall locked the alley door and told the boys to go on into the lunch-room. When they had done so he locked the door into the back room behind them. They seated themselves on stools and smiled at Hall. Hall's expression remained blank.

"It sure is good stuff, ain't it, Fat?" Chick enthused.

"I guess it's all right," Hall grudgingly agreed.

"It's worth more'n a grand," Chick said.

"I'll make it bring me twenty-five hundred," Hall gloated.

"You wanna buy some more?" Chick asked.

"Buy some more what?"

"Some more booze."

89

"I ain't bought no booze."

Chick laughed uneasily. Hall had a peculiar expression on his face, and his assertion had sounded ominous.

"Well, whisky then," Chick amended. "Maybe you don't call good whisky booze."

"I ain't bought no whisky," Hall said.

"What's the joke?" asked Chick.

"If you guys want to order anything you better hurry. I eat my supper at nine o'clock, an' I hate like hell to get up an' cook for customers while I'm eatin'."

"We ain't hungry," Chick said. "We don't wanna eat, do we, Benny?"

"No," said Benny. "We ain't hungry, I guess."

"Well, then, what can I do for you?"

"Nothin', I guess," Chick replied. "Just give us the dough an' we'll call it square."

"Dough? What dough?" Hall's eyes were dangerously steady as he glared at Chick.

Chick tried to laugh, and made a funny noise in high falsetto. Benny looked bewildered, blinking, with his mouth open. Chick tried to keep his voice steady as he said:

"You're a great joker, ain't you, Fat?"

"No," said Hall. "No, I never joke. What can I do for you?" He kept repeating the question, thinking it the height of sarcasm to pronounce what he considered cultured words of politeness in his oily, bantering tone.

90

"Give us the grand an' we'll shove off," Chick
said. He was afraid now. Fat was double-crossing
him, and he hated to admit that it had been possible.
He didn't want to believe that any one could make
a chump of him. Especially was it humiliating to
have this happen before Benny. Had he been
double-crossed alone he could have explained to the
gang with credit to himself. Chick liked to appear
as important as possible, to seem heroic to the little
fellows. And here was Benny, one of his worshipers, seeing Fat Hall make a fool of him. He
couldn't let Hall get away with it.

"Give us the grand," he said, trying to sound firm.

"What grand?" Hall asked. "Are you tryin' to
be funny?"

"The grand you owe us for the booze," Chick
specified. "We want it so we can go."

"Well, go on then—I ain't stoppin' you. I don't
owe you nothin'. You better beat it 'fore I get sore."

"You ain't gonna pay us what you owe us?"

"I don't owe you nothin'."

"You owe us a thousand bucks," Benny broke in.

"You keep your trap shut, kid. You wanna keep
outta trouble, don'tcha? You don't wanna get hurt,
do you?"

"No," said Benny, "I don't wanna get hurt. But
I want the dough."

"You ain't gonna get no dough offa me," Hall
shouted. "You can't do a damn thing about it,
neither. You better mope."

"You gotta give us the dough," Chick insisted doggedly.

"I'll give you hell!   Beat it—'fore I get rough."

"We ain't afraid of you, you fat hog," Chick defied.

"Oh, yeah?   You ain't, hunh?"

"No, we ain't"—a bit weakly.

"You ain't gonna cop a mope?"

"Not without that grand."   Chick was aware that once he was out of the place he would have no further hope of getting the money.   He was determined to stick it out as long as possible.

"We'll see about that," Hall said grimly.   He reached under the counter, and when his arm reappeared they saw the sinister razor-sharp blade of the huge cleaver in his hand.   Chick and Benny had both heard the story of the man on the Barbary Coast. They knew what he kept the cleaver for.   And he was fingering the blade suggestively, leering across the counter at Chick.

"Maybe you punks heard what happened in 'Frisco one night?" he said softly, smiling obscenely with his thick, soft lips.

"You wouldn't—"

"Oh, no?   Well, I guess I would.   You ain't so much.   I'd just tell the cops it was self-defense." He took a firmer grip on the handle of the cleaver, and raised it slightly as he looked calculatingly at Chick's head.

"You gonna beat it?"

92

Chick had turned white, and he was trembling a bit as he stared at the uplifting blade. Benny was looking on in terror. Chick backed away from the counter toward the door, staring fascinatedly at the gleaming blade. As he reached the door Benny joined him and they went out together. On the street something smashed suddenly against the back of Benny's neck, and he reached back and found that Hall had hurled an egg. His neck and back were messy with it. He drew his fingers back, and the slimy white of the egg dripped from them disgustingly. Suddenly his face flamed with rage. For the first time in his life he burst out in a passion of hot anger at some one who had humiliated and scorned him. He whirled on his heels and started back towards the lunch room.

"The dirty son of a bitch," he snarled. "I'm goin' back in there an' clean up on him."

"He'll kill you," cried Chick, seizing Benny by the arm. "Wait, Benny. I gotta better idea. We'll get Eddie an' Spike."

As they went around to the alley for the roadster they heard the heavy laughter of Fat Hall, a throaty sound like the cry of a maddened hog.

"We'll get him," Chick said. "He won't laugh long."

93

V

WHEN Chick told Eddie and Spike what had happened in Fat Hall's lunch-room the two gangsters leapt from their flivver and swore lustily.

"No fat slob like him can put anything like that over on *us* an' get away with it," Spike blustered. "What the hell does he think we are?"

"We'll go an' clean up on him," snarled Eddie, fingering his pearl tie-pin.

"Damn right we will," Spike enthusiastically seconded. Chick laid a restraining hand on Spike's arm.

"Don't make so damn much noise about it. We gotta sneak up on him. Me an' Benny'll go in an' give him one more chance to come across. If he don't, then you guys rush the joint. We'll take all he owes us an' then some if he's got the dough in the joint."

"He's got plenty o' dough," Spike said, his eyes gleaming. "He just about runs things here at the beach."

"We'll mess him up," said Eddie.

Benny's neck still tingled from the smash of the egg. He felt as though the bootlegger had spit on him. It had been an insult, all the more ignominious because Chick McTeague had been there to

94

see it. He wanted to go back and smash eggs all over the ugly fat face of Hall. He'd like to go back and smear eggs and mustard and catsup and all the other gooey things all over Hall's leering face, and in his hair. Benny agreed heartily with Eddie's suggestion that they mess Hall up.

But Chick was the leader. He'd do what Chick said, and Hall would get plenty of what he deserved.

"Let's go," said Chick. "Come on, Benny; you an' me'll go tell that fat louse what's what."

Eddie and Spike got back into the flivver and drove slowly behind the walking pair, a cavalcade of indignation. Spike and Eddie were thinking only of the money; Chick had his position as leader to uphold, his ego to feed; Benny had forgotten all about the money, for the back of his neck was still sticky with egg.

When they came in sight of Hall's Spike parked the machine. He and Eddie sat and watched while Chick and Benny entered the lunch-room, then they got out and walked to the building, keeping out of sight a few feet from the entrance. Hall's lunch-room was on a side street, away from the bright lights of the amusement zone. The two watchers were indistinct in the shadows, their felt hats pulled low over their eyes, their hands gripping the black-jacks in their pockets. They peered cautiously through the window and saw Hall look up and snarl at Benny and Chick.

In the lunch-room Hall was sneering from the corner of his mouth:

"Ain't had enough, hunh? Well, the motto o' this joint is 'Service with a Smile'—but to you it'll be with a big laugh."

He rose slowly from his stool and reached under the counter.

"Wait a minute," said Chick, "I wanta talk to you."

"I ain't got nothin' to say to you punks—nothin' at all."

"Well," said Chick, "we just wanta give you a chance, that's all. You shell out what you owe us an' we'll let you be. If you don't come across we're gonna wreck the joint."

"Oh, yeah? You're gettin' ambitious, ain't you? Well, you better clear out before I make Hamburger outta you."

Benny was standing before the counter, and near him was a large bottle of catsup. He eyed it calculatingly. The catsup, he thought, would smear nicely over Hall's fat head. Better than the egg. It would sure mess him up. He began to slide his hand over toward the bottle of catsup.

"You ain't gonna come across?" Chick asked ominously.

"I ain't givin' you nothin'," Hall repeated.

Chick whistled. As Eddie and Spike rushed in Chick's fist suddenly shot out and smashed against the fat man's flabby jowl, connecting with a strange

96

smacking noise that ended in a pop as the air was forced from Hall's mouth. Instantly Hall changed. No longer did his flesh sag in immobile lethargy. The muscles seemed to leap out and absorb the fat, so that he was a giant of action, incredibly swift for a man of his build. The cleaver seemed to materialize magically in his hand. Chick leapt back. Eddie and Spike swung their black-jacks, Eddie being slightly to the right of Hall. Benny grasped the catsup bottle. Swiftly as the flight of a silver bird Hall raised the cleaver. Benny saw it poised in its momentary pause between ascent and descent, heard the horrible swish of air as it flashed down, heard a crunching noise and a gasp at his side, and let fly with the bottle. The bottle smashed against the head of Hall, its red contents streaming ludicrously over the face and neck of the bootlegger, blinding his animal-eyes, dripping over his nose and into his panting mouth. Benny laughed. The bootlegger looked so funny there, slumped on his stool, his back against a shelf of pies and cakes, the huge cleaver in his hand and the red catsup streaming all over him like thick blood. He looked like a big wounded beast, a wild pig, puffing and snorting there, trying to catch his breath. 'He wants to kill me,' thought Benny delightedly. 'I got him mad as hell. He can't do nothin', an' it makes him mad. He's all out of wind.'

Hall was stunned by the blow. A small, jagged fragment of glass was imbedded in his skull. He was making no effort to raise the cleaver again. He just sat and looked stupid, the catsup splashed all over him. 'Guess I scared him,' Benny exulted. 'He won't cut nobody up now.'

The entire action had taken but a second. Chick McTeague had backed to the wall, and Benny could see Spike Davis moving back beside him. Benny didn't turn. He was fascinated by the sight of the catsup-covered, stunned bootlegger. He was glorying in his new-found strength, the strength that had put Fat Hall out of commission. But he heard Spike Davis cry out:

"God! Ain't this a mess!" His voice was low and scared.

"Let's get outta here," said Chick. "We don't wanta get mixed up in anything like this."

Benny laughed and pointed at Hall.

"I hit him with the catsup," he said. "Look at him now! All red like blood. An' the big bum was goin' to cut us with that thing."

He wondered suddenly why Spike and Chick didn't laugh, why they looked so white and scared. Why did they look that way at Hall? He was nothing to be afraid of now. He was still in a fog, still gasping on the stool. But Benny's eyes suddenly became focused on the cleaver. It was red with a redness that was not catsup, and mixed with the red was something stringy, something that looked like hair. He stared at it. Something was wrong. A premonition of horror swept over him as he turned

98

to Chick and Spike, and when his gaze followed
theirs to the floor he recoiled, sickened by what he
saw. Eddie Sheehan lay there, his right arm bent
under him, his blood staining the floor and soaking
into his clothing. His head was split open from the
top of his skull to his nose. The blood was spurting
out, along with a mass of something thicker than
blood. It was running over the dead youth's face,
hiding the staring eyes, filling the open mouth . . .

Benny gasped, and suddenly his stomach seemed
to turn over within him. With his back against the
counter he slid to the floor. He sat there, hiding
from the thing on the floor, his head in his arms,
shutting out his first sight of violent death. He did
not see Chick and Spike run from the building. He
did not see the officers rush in. He knew, vaguely,
that some one was fighting, some one was cursing and
threatening, telling the cops that they couldn't take
him away. It was Fat Hall defying the police, but
Benny felt that he could not raise his head to see
what was going on.

They had to lock Hall in the jail hospital, but
they threw Benny into a cell and left him there. All
night he was tortured by the vision of a split skull
oozing blood and brains. Over and over he relived
the scene. It became so graphic that he began to
imagine himself in Eddie's place. He could almost
feel the sinking of the blade into his own brain.
He wanted to scream, to cry. He woke from one
short nightmare crying out despairingly for Lou

Warren. She could soothe him, cuddle him against her breast and comfort him.

"Lou—Lou," he called. "Help me." . . .

But a guard was passing along the corridor outside the bars, making his hourly rounds, watching suspiciously for anything unusual, anything that would give him the excuse to break the monotony of his night-vigil by snarling a warning or a threat to a prisoner.

"Pipe down in there," he snapped. "Wanna wake everybody up? You'll get help to-morrer. Yeah, plenty o' help. Keep yer mouth shut an' go to sleep."

"All right," said Benny, thoroughly awake now. He heard the guard walk on, heard him bumming a cigarette from a wakeful prisoner further along the line of cells.

'I'm in jail,' he thought. 'In jail . . . in jail . . . in jail.' He was trying to comprehend his position, the full horror of what had happened, where he was. Jail was a place to be afraid of, a place where things happened to you and where you had to eat bread and water and be locked up in dark dungeons. He wasn't in a dark dungeon now, and that rather puzzled him. He was in a dank cell, lying on a wooden shelf, with a blanket over him that tickled his skin and smelled of disinfectant. Light from an electric light shone through the bars of his door, and cast shadows of bars on the wall at the foot of his bunk. 'I'm in jail,' he repeated to himself. 'My God, I'm in jail . . . in jail.'

And he thought again, 'What happened to Chick and Spike—and to *Eddie?*' The vision of Eddie's skull returned, and he writhed in vicarious torture as he saw the gleaming cleaver, bigger and ever bigger, sinking deeper and deeper into an endless skull . . .

VI

L UMPY, poorly cooked mush, hard bread and acrid chicory, with neither sugar nor milk, for breakfast. Benny didn't care. He couldn't eat, couldn't have eaten ripe strawberries and rich cream, or ham and eggs if they had been brought to him. He was sick, horribly, despairingly sick. His stomach felt detached from his insides, and his head ached dully. He had not slept more than an hour all night, and his fitful naps had been hideous with dreams of Eddie's death. He was afraid. He did not know what they were holding him for, how long they would keep him. At ten o'clock his name was called, and he was told a visitor was waiting to see him.

It was his father. August looked worn and ill. He trembled as he peered at Benny through the heavy mesh of the screen that separated the visitors from the prisoners in the narrow visiting room. Benny spoke first, feeling that he must defend himself in some way.

"I didn't do nothin'," he said weakly.

"I ain't here to bawl you out, Benny. I just want to know how it happened."

"I don't know," Benny said. "I don't know— really."

"It was Chick McTeague got you into it, wasn't it?"

"Chick's all right," Benny asserted, showing a bit of spirit for the first time. "It wasn't his fault."

"He knows more'n you do," August said.

"It wasn't his fault," Benny repeated.

"He ain't goin' to help you. He won't say anything to help you."

"He can't. He don't know anything."

"I want to know how it happened," August repeated. "I can't help you unless I know about it."

"I don't even know what they pinched me for," Benny said.

"They're goin' to charge you with assault with intent to kill while committin' a highway robbery."

"Intent to kill? Highway robbery? Why—they *can't*." Benny was astounded, frightened by the length and seriousness of the charge. "They can't do it," he repeated.

"They can," August said in a patiently hopeless voice. "They can do anything. Hall's goin' to say you tried to hold him up—you an' your partner—an' he killed your partner in self-defense when the two of you attacked him."

"He's a liar," Benny said.

"I know it, but he's got pull an' he can prove it if we let his case go to court. He's got the cut on his head to prove he was hit."

"We never tried to hold him up," Benny said.

"I know it. I know what happened."

"You know?"

103

"Sure. Ethel saw you take the whisky from the basement. She was in her room. She didn't go out yesterday afternoon."

"An' she'll squawk?"

"She hates you, Benny."

"Can't you talk to her?"

"Chick McTeague already got to her."

"Chick McTeague? What for?"

"Alderman McTeague wants me to sell whisky, Benny. He wants to steal it from the warehouse."

"What's that got to do with Ethel?"

"Ethel's been up to things we didn't know about, I guess. She's been runnin' out with Chick a little. He's turned her head. Showed her how we'd make a lot of money. Ethel likes money all right, I guess. Her mother backs her up."

"What you gonna do?"

"If I don't let McTeague have his way Ethel is goin' to tell about the whisky. She's goin' to say we're bootleggers. She's goin' to say you tried to kill Hall so you could steal some booze from his place."

"Tried to steal it! Why, what the hell— We *put* it there!

"I know you did, Benny. But she's goin' to say you tried to steal it. Hall is goin' to swear the stuff was always there. He can prove it, too. He's got receipts to show he bought a lot before Prohibition."

"But why the hell? How's Hall gonna do all this? Ain't he arrested?"

104

"I'll try to tell you about it, Benny. They're ready to charge Hall with murder. His defense is that you an' Eddie Sheehan tried to highjack him an' kill him, an' he had to fight for his life. He'll swear out a warrant for you. But if I do what McTeague wants he'll square it for you. He'll get the case against Hall dropped, an' Hall won't say nothin' about you."

"How they gonna square it?"

"McTeague knows how. He's got it all planned, Benny. Hall will be glad to get out of it without a trial. He won't even make a charge against you."

"If you do what McTeague wants then the rap against Hall will be dropped, an' he won't have to frame me up. That what you mean?"

"Yeah, that's it, Benny."

"An' what you gonna do?"

"I told McTeague it was all right. He's gettin' his men to take the stuff from the warehouse to-night. He had the guards all fixed long ago. I got carpenters workin' in the restaurant now. We'll be closed a week. When we open up we'll be runnin' a speakeasy. There'll be a cigar store in front. There'll be a steel door between it an' the joint. Everything was all planned, ready for the workmen."

"Gee, he works fast, don't he?"

"He has to," said August. "There's too much booze bein' taken from warehouses. The Government is goin' to make a change pretty soon. Goin' to cut out some of the warehouses. There's more'n three hundred now, an' it's too easy for booze to get out. McTeague wants to get plenty while he's got the chance."

"Won't he get caught?"

"No, I guess not. He's pretty careful. We all know he's behind all this, but nobody could prove it. I own the place, an' I own the liquor. Chick's goin' to be in the place, but he'll be on my payroll. That's how McTeague will get his end. I'll pay Chick for bein' a waiter, an' Chick turns it over to his old man. Only thing is, old man McTeague is in a big hurry now, an' he might slip up on something. I hope not."

"You don't want to do it, do you, Dad?"

Benny looked anxiously through the screen at his father. He could see, dimly through the haze of the mesh, the hopeless grief on the face of the old man. For a moment he caught a flash of what life had done to his father, felt a sudden tie of understanding between them. Had the old man, also, suffered under the tyranny of Angela and Ethel? Mentally he reached out and sympathetically clasped the bald-headed, sad-faced man who had meant so little to him through his young life, but who now loomed so utterly necessary.

"You better not do it," he said. "I don't want you to do it. You don't want to do it."

August didn't answer at once, and almost instantly Benny forgot his moment of sympathy and became fearful that his father would accept his abnegation. He couldn't stand the thought of staying in jail, couldn't go through with it.   If it would free him from the horror of those bars and stone walls and the rattle of huge keys, no sacrifice was too great. He could accept his father's ransom, could cheerfully see the old man going into something he hated, if only he could be free.   He must be freed at once.

"I got to do it," said August quietly, sensing all that was in Benny's mind.   "Anyway, it's too late to back out now.   They got everything fixed."

Benny was relieved.   He was humanly selfish, and after all it was himself who mattered most.   But with the relief from anxiety came another wave of sympathy for his father.   'He looks ten years older,' he thought.   'The old guy must be worried.'

"Maybe everything'll be all right," he said. "Maybe you'll make a lot of dough."

"Maybe I will," August agreed with no enthusiasm.

"It ain't no disgrace, anyway," Benny reasoned. "Lots of people are doin' it."

"No," said August.   "No, it ain't no disgrace, I guess.   That's what Angela and Ethel said."

"Damn Ethel!" Benny snapped.   "What you gonna do about her?"

"Buy her some new clothes," said August.   "New dresses an' hats, an' a new piano—an' maybe a car. That's what she wants.   That's what she said she needed when she told me I wasn't givin' her the

107

things other girls have. Girls need things, Benny.
Girls need lots o' things. Angela says they need
more now'n they used to need. I guess she knows.
Ethel don't like to look poor before the other girls."

"The dirty slut," Benny almost whispered. "Always wantin' her own way an' never carin' about anybody else."

"I never heard you talk that way about her before.
She's your sister, Benny."

"You never heard me talk about her before 'cause
she was always doin' all the talkin'. She always
hated me, an' I hate her. Damn it, she never give
me a chance. You never knew what she done to me
—her an' her old lady. You let 'em run things to
suit 'emselves. Why didn't you ever stop 'em?"
Benny's welled-up bitterness was finding astonish-
ing expression.

"I married Ethel's mother," said August sadly,
"an' I guess I got to treat her right."

"I guess I never counted, hunh?" Benny reflected
bitterly.

Old August hung his head for a moment, then
looked up with the pain of frustration in his eyes.

"Benny, you mustn't be too hard on me. I know
I ain't done all I should for you. I done the best I
could. Your poor mother passed away when you
were born, an', Benny—I just couldn't bring you up
alone. I had to get a woman for you. I had to,
Benny. Maybe you'll hate me because you didn't
have everything, but I didn't know. I want you to

understand that I married Angela just because you needed a mother."

"A hell of a mother!"

"Maybe, Benny, but I couldn't look around an' pick one out. I was workin' all the time, an' she was already there nursin' you. She was a good mother to her own, Benny. We got to give her credit for that. I been with her a good many years, an' I understand things better now. I know that a woman can be a good mother to her own an' still be a worthless stepmother. It's nature, Benny. It don't do you no good to know that now, but you shouldn't hate Angela for lovin' Ethel."

"I guess you didn't know," Benny conceded. "I guess maybe you was a little bit afraid of her, too— like I was afraid of Ethel."

"I wasn't afraid," August explained. "I was just tryin' to be fair to her. It wasn't her fault I married her."

"She wanted a good home. She didn't love you."

"Maybe not. Anyway, we got to make the best of it. We got to get you out of jail first thing."

"When you gonna get me out?"

"It won't be long. Few days, I guess. Soon's Hall's case is dismissed. There ain't any charge against you yet. They're just holding you as a material witness."

"Well, get me out soon's you can. It's a hell of a place."

"I know. I'll do my best. Want anything to eat sent in?"

"Maybe I can eat now," said Benny doubtfully. "Yeah, I guess I can eat. Send in some smokes too."

When his father had gone the jail didn't look quite so drear. He would get out soon, and the thought of freedom made him feel better.

VII

THE passing of a week brought strange and disquieting news to Benny. Fat Hall had been released from the hospital, but he was not in jail. He had arranged bail, and was free to go as he pleased. Benny reflected bitterly that he, who had done nothing but demand his rights from the bootlegger, must remain behind the bars while the man who had committed a cold-blooded murder was on the street.

Benny's nightmares had not ceased. The horror in the lunch-room had photographed itself indelibly on his mind and he could not shake it off. At night he would wake suddenly from a dream of carnage to find his entire body tense and clammy with sweat. He would lie there trembling, trying to clear his mind of the dream so that he might sleep again. During the day he kept to himself, worrying himself to a shaky wreck. He became enervated and nervous, his eyes red and heavy from lack of sleep. He could not read, nor could he become interested in the boisterous games of the prisoners. His mind had drawn into itself, wrapping itself around the hideous image of Eddie's gashed head and the bloody cleaver in Hall's enormous hand. At the end of the week he had lost twenty pounds.

Only one of the other prisoners had evinced any interest in him. This man, a big-nosed, pasty-faced individual who always talked in low tones as though he were imparting secrets, had watched Benny for three days before he finally spoke. Benny encouraged him but slightly, and the man left him to himself and continued to watch from a distance. Benny was too deeply engrossed in his problems to wonder about the man's strange interest.

When Lou Warren finally came she found a strange Benny, a Benny with wanly sunken cheeks and quavering voice. She tried to see him clearly through the screen, and what she saw alarmed her.

"Benny, you look ill. Aren't you getting enough food?"

"Sure, I get plenty. The old man sends stuff in." He didn't think it necessary to tell her that he could not eat, that he gave away most of the food brought to him.

"You look bad, though. Maybe it's this screen. I wish we could talk somewhere else. Benny—I have some bad news."

Benny slumped a bit on the bench on which the prisoners had to sit back of the visiting screen. Bad news could mean but one thing—more suffering.

"Ain't they gonna let me out?" he murmured.

"It's not that, Benny. Oh, Benny, I've got to go away. I've got to go to work."

"Work?"

"My father is gone."

"Gone? You mean—"

"He's disappeared, left us flat. He sold the barber shop and ran away with the money. A little money was too much for him."

Benny could only stare at her dumbly. He sensed the note of hopeless resignation in her words, but there seemed nothing to say. She had begun to cry softly, and that hurt him more than anything. He wanted to touch her, to comfort her. The screen was a frustration that maddened him. He seemed caught in a cage that held him helpless, futile. Lou strove to regain her composure.

"Benny, he sold his barber shop to Fat Hall."

"My God, Lou—why?" Fat Hall and Alderman McTeague and all the other big shots seemed to be rolling over him and his love, crushing them.

"Hall wants to leave the beach. He's starting a business in the shop. I suppose you know what that means."

"Yeah—I know. I gotta get outta here, Lou. I gotta get out."

"You will, Benny."

"Sure—I guess I will, Lou. It's tough, kid. My God, it's hell."

"You'll get out. It'll turn out right. We'll be happy together, Benny."

"I know we will, kid. I know we'll be happy— when I get out. I wish I could get out."

"Don't worry, Benny. It won't do you any good

to worry. I know it's hard. I wish I could help you."

"Do you love me, Lou?"

"Of course I do. Oh, honey, you know I do."

"I know you do. Don't cry, kid. Please don't cry."

"I can't help it, Benny. Oh, this screen!"

"Don't cry, Lou—please."

"Benny—*you're* crying!"

"No, Lou, I ain't. I—ain't bawlin'. I wouldn't bawl."

"You are, Benny."

"You said you're goin' away."

"I have to, Benny. Mother's going to some of her people."

"You goin' with her, Lou?"

"They won't have room for me. I'm going to New York and work. I'll come back, though."

"You'll sure come back?"

"I'll come back just as soon as you're on your feet. We can marry—just as soon as you make good."

"I'll work hard, Lou. You can come back pretty soon, I guess."

"I hope so, Benny."

"Don't cry, Lou."

"I won't in a minute. I can't help it now."

"Your lips're tremblin'."

"No, Benny—don't make your voice sound like that. It makes me cry."

"I don't want you to cry."

"You're crying, Benny. I know you are."

"Gee, Lou, we're both bawlin' like a coupla babies.
It seems to fill me all up inside when you cry."

"Benny—oh, this screen, this screen—Benny, put
your face up against the screen. Maybe I can touch
you just a little."

"This way? . . . Gee, Lou, I *can* feel your face
against mine . . . just a little bit . . . Let's press
harder . . . now—I can feel your face through the
screen."

"Oh, Benny, Benny!"

"Don't, kid; if the screw hears you poundin' on
the screen he'll chase you."

"I didn't know I loved you so much."

"I guess I didn't either. Gee, Lou—I guess we
are in love, ain't we?"

"Oh, Benny! That screen made funny little black
squares all over the side of your face."

"Gee—yours too. You better wipe it off, kid."

"There—is it off?"

"Let's see—sure, it's all off, Lou . . . Gee, that
powder smells good.   Blow some through the
screen."

"There! I knew you'd sneeze, Benny."

"It got up my nose."

"You sneezed so funny!"

"I like to see you smile, kid."

"You keep smiling, Benny. Everything will be
all right. I'll write every week."

"Won't I see you again?"

"I'm going to-morrow, Benny. I've got to get to work as soon as I can—before the money gives out."

"Gee, Lou, I'm sorry."

"Don't worry, Benny. Promise me you won't let yourself worry about *me*."

"I can't promise that, Lou."

"Benny, please."

"Aw right, kid. I'll get along. You write every week."

"I will, Benny. Here comes that officer, Benny. I suppose my half hour is up."

"Good-by, Lou."

"All right, officer, I'll go.—Good-by, Benny."

"Take it easy, kid. Don't start cryin' again."

"No, Benny—I'm just—wiping the powder—away from—my eyes."

"Kiss me good-by."

"Oh, Benny—"

"You *could* feel my lips—couldn't you?"

"Oh, yes, Benny—I did. I felt them."

"I felt yours, too."

"That officer is coming back. Good-by, Benny."

"Good-by, kid. Take it easy."

She was gone, and God knew when he would see her again. Back in the jail "tank" he sat by himself on a bench against the wall and thought of what she had said. Hall, the fat hog who had killed Eddie Sheehan, was to be his neighbor. That meant that Hall would want to rule the whole district. He would want everything for himself. He'd try to control the bootlegging business. Benny's father would be his rival—bossed by Alderman McTeague. Chick McTeague would really be manager of the new speakeasy. Chick was Hall's enemy. He must be—after that night at Lido. There'd be trouble sure.

'I gotta get out,' he thought miserably. 'Gotta get out 'fore somethin' happens.' He did not know what he could do to prevent trouble if he did get out, but in jail he felt so impotent that he imagined freedom would give him power to do anything.

'Lou's goin' away,' his mind sobbed. 'New York. I gotta get out. Why can't I get out? Hall's out. Fat bastard. He's out. He's out. He's out. Where the hell did her old man go? Got a little dough an' beat it. He got the dough dough dough, he got the dough. He had some o' my booze. Some o' my booze. Some o' *my* booze. Fat Hall will cop it. Hall gets it all Hall gets everything Hall gets all Hall all Hall all . . . Damn Ed Warren makin' Lou go to New York. Damn the louse . . . no good louse . . . louse . . . louse . . . hurtin' Lou . . . Lou Lou LOuLouLou—Oh, Lou! . . . Gotta get out an' find her. Gotta get out gotta get out out out out . . . Hell! Damn! Hell damn helldamn helldamn. . . . *Christ!* I'm goin' bugs!' —"Well, whadda *you* want?"

The last words were addressed aloud to some one

who had touched his shoulder. It was the big-nosed man who had spoken to him before. The man was large and seemed to completely obscure Benny as he stood before him.

"You worried, kid? You been actin' funny," said the intruder.

Benny was sorry he had been so brusque. "No," he said, "I ain't worried. None at all. What makes you think I'm worried?"

"You been actin' like it had the best of you. Something's on your mind. You look bad."

"I don't feel very good," Benny admitted.

"I been watchin' you. You don't eat, an' you don't look like you sleep. I been feelin' sorry for you. This your first drop?"

"First what?"

"First fall—first pinch?"

"Oh, yes. Yes, this is my first, all right."

"Well, take it easy. Anything I can do to help? Want any readin'?"

"No, I don't feel like readin'."

"A guy what can't read pulls a tough bit. Sometimes a guy in stir goes bugs 'cause he can't read. Guys in stir read a lot."

"I can't read," Benny said.

"Ain't you been to school?"

"I can read all right," said Benny. "I just don't feel like it."

"Sure, I know. Can't put your mind on it. Well, maybe I can help you."

118

The man was sympathetic. Benny liked him and told him the whole story. It made him feel better to have somebody to talk to. When he had finished telling about Hall and Eddie and how it affected him the man looked thoughtful a moment. Then he patted Benny on the back and looked sympathetic. He knew how to look sympathetic.

"An' you can't sleep, hunh?" he asked.

"Gee," said Benny, shuddering a bit, "I can't keep from thinkin' 'bout that guy with the smashed head. I can *feel* it."

"Yeah, I know. It gets a guy, it does."

"You ever been like that?"

"Sure have, pal."

"You don't look worried. I wish I could forget it."

"I guess maybe we can fix that— What's your name?"

"Benny Wagner."

"Mine's Murphy. Jew Murphy. I'm part kike an' part mick. Un'erstand?"

He seemed to challenge Benny to criticize the combination. Benny nodded his head.

"You're a right guy, I c'n see that," Jew Murphy went on. "I c'n fix you up great, too. What cell you lock in?"

"Forty-two."

"Anybody lockin' with you?"

"No."

"O.K. I'll fix it with the head trusty to put me

in there with you. Don't say nothin' to anybody, see. I'll move in there to-night an' show you somethin'."

"What you gonna do?"

"Make you forget that bump-off, see. I got some medicine. You'll sleep an' feel good."

"Aw right. I guess you know."

"Sure I do. Wait till to-night, see. Don't say nothin', see. Now I'll cop a mope. See you to-night."

Half an hour later Benny saw Jew Murphy in confidential conversation with the head trusty. A few minutes later he saw the Irish Jew moving his few belongings into cell number forty-two.

'Guess he's just a nut,' thought Benny, 'but he can't hurt me none. We can talk. That'll pass the time. Gee, I wish they'd let me out.'

VIII

AT five o'clock a bell clanged and the prisoners
were herded into their cells for the night.
Most of them were glad another day was gone, but
with the characteristic reluctance of men under re-
strictions to conform willingly to rules they slouched
sullenly to their doors, sneering and uttering cat-
calls as the guards urged them to hurry.

Night in prison is a strange thing. Life is different then from the nervous exuberance of the prison
day. The night-life of the prisoner is introverted.
After the customary night meal of foodstuffs cached
in their cells the men become thoughtful. Those
who lock alone read if they have light. Some of
them write letters. Others merely rest on their
bunks and think. Those who lock two in a cell sit
on the lower bunk, smoking cigarettes and talking in
low tones. They reminisce, evoking good times of
the past. They look into the future, planning glories
yet to be. Cell-mates become confidential, telling
each other their dreams and ambitions without the
fear of derision by the mob that inhibits them by
day. Men who by day live the extravert life of
primitives become human at night. Their cells are
their little homes. Perhaps the guards do make

121

their hourly rounds, their ears attuned for suspicious sounds, but who can say that the man outside whose home is his castle will not this very night find the Prohibition agents at his door, demanding and forcing entrance without legal sanction?

Turn the page and see the other side of the picture; the hardened criminal locking with the tyro— Jew Murphy in a four-by-ten cell with Benny Wagner.

Benny drew a box from under the bunk. It was the daily box of eatables sent in by old August, who could not see his son because the jail rules said that the same person could not visit a prisoner more than once a month. Jew Murphy became interested when he saw the box.

"What you got there?" he asked.

"Good stuff, I guess. Old man brings a box every day. I ain't had no appetite though."

"Well, *I* sure can eat."

Benny opened the box on the bed and Jew Murphy dug in.

"Fried chicken, hunh? Great stuff. It's the money, all right."

"Yeah—fried chicken is O.K."

"Why don'tcha eat some then?"

"Maybe I will. Yeah—guess I will." Benny brought forth a leg and bit into it.

"You oughtta eat, kid."

"I guess I can eat to-night. I ain't so lonesome."

"Sure—you been thinkin' too much."

"It's good chicken."

They ate all the chicken and started on the pie. When they had eaten the whole pie they sat and looked at the box a moment. There were some sandwiches in it, but they didn't eat any. Jew Murphy brought out a pack of cigarettes. They were expensive cigarettes and had a sweetish taste. Benny liked them. He wondered how Jew Murphy could afford them in jail. After they had smoked awhile Jew Murphy got up and held a small mirror through the bars of the door. He turned it both ways so he could see what was going on in the corridor. He put the mirror back in his pocket and sat down.

"The screw's comin' now, makin' his rounds."

"He always does," said Benny.

"Hell—don't I know that? But it's Bill Jensen. He's O.K."

"Comes around every hour, don't he?"

"Yeah, but he don't see nothin'."

"Don't he? That's all right, I guess."

The guard passed, turned and came back to the door.

"Moved, hunh, Murphy?"

"Yeah, Bill. Doubled up with a friend."

"That's good," said the guard. "That's good, Murphy."

"You said it, Bill. That guy I locked with was no good."

"He was a louse," said the guard.

"That's right. I guess you know, eh? You want a sandwich?"

"Sure. What kind you got?"

"Ham—"

"I like ham."

"Swiss cheese—"

"I don't care so much—"

"Swiss cheese is good. Got mustard on it."

"I like ham."

"We got salami, too, but the Swiss cheese is better."

"I like ham. Swiss cheese isn't—"

"Good Swiss cheese is hard to get. This is good Swiss cheese."

The guard took the Swiss-cheese sandwich and began to eat. Jew Murphy laughed and held a ham sandwich through the bars. The guard took it and grinned.

"Tryin' to kid me, hunh? Well, you're a card all right."

"I know you don't like Swiss cheese, Bill."

"It's good, all right, but I like ham."

"Well, eat 'em both. We aim to please."

"You're a card," the keeper repeated, laughing.

"I know my friends," said Jew Murphy.

"I'll be back later," the guard said. They heard him walking down the corridor. He tramped heavily so they could hear how far away he was. Pretty soon they heard the clang of steel on steel as he closed a door. They knew he had left the tank.

Murphy removed a small black box from his pocket. He opened it and Benny saw something shiny inside. It was a hypodermic needle. Jew Murphy laid it on the bed and began to cook up a shot of morphine. He placed some of the white stuff in a spoon with some water, then held a lighted match under the spoon. When the mixture was hot he drew it into the hypodermic and pressed it into his arm. He rubbed his arm and smiled at Benny. Benny didn't say anything. He'd never seen it done before, but he knew all about it. He'd known people who used it.

Jew Murphy cooked another spoonful of the white stuff and told Benny to roll up his sleeve. Benny was scared. He didn't know what it would do to him.

"I'm afraid it'll make me sick. I never took none before."

"Your ticker O.K.?"

"What?"

"Your heart—you gotta good heart?"

"Oh, sure, my heart—my *ticker* is all right. Yeah —I gotta extra strong one."

"Well, then, it won't hurt you."

Jew Murphy rolled Benny's sleeve up, and Benny didn't protest. Jew Murphy thought it was all right, so it must be. Jew Murphy was a big shot.

"It'll make you feel good," said Murphy. "It'll make you forget your troubles. You won't think no more about that gee with the smashed top."

"Aw right, then."

Benny winced as the needle bored into his flesh, but it only hurt for a second. After that he didn't feel anything but a pleasant tickle. He sat on the bed and waited to see what would happen. He thought, 'Dope makes a guy feel funny right away. I'll feel it in a minute. I'll have funny dreams. Wonder what I'll dream? I'll feel happy. I'll wanta sing an' laugh. It'll make me feel like I'm in heaven.' But he sat there and didn't feel anything. He sat very still and waited. He didn't feel happy like they said it made them feel. He just felt like he didn't want to move. Jew Murphy gave him another cigarette. They sat and smoked awhile, but Benny didn't feel any different. He was puzzled. He didn't even feel like talking. Jew Murphy had been talking, but Benny hadn't paid any attention. He smoked his cigarette and watched the smoke curling up in the dim light that shone through the bars. The smoke from Murphy's cigarette merged with the smoke from his, and there was a sort of floating haze drifting through the door. The haze was white, but when he looked hard at it it didn't seem real. It looked like it shouldn't be there. Nothing should be there.

"How you feel?" asked Murphy. "Get a kick out of it?"

"I feel just the same," Benny said. His voice was very low, but he heard it fill the cell and smash back against his ears.

An hour later the guard came along again, and Jew Murphy talked to him. Benny took a sandwich from the box and held it toward the door. His hand seemed to leap out from him, trying to fly.

"Have a sandwich," he said. "It's ham."

"What's the matter with the kid?" asked the guard.

"He's O.K.," said Murphy. "Feelin' great."

The guard laughed, and Murphy joined in. The guard took the sandwich and laughed again. Benny didn't see anything to laugh at. All he'd done was hand the guard a sandwich, and they were laughing at him.

"Whatcha laughin' at?" he asked dully.

"It's all right, kid. You just dropped all the ham outta the sandwich an' give Bill the dry bread."

The guard slipped a small package through the bars to Murphy.

"Be careful," he warned. "I'm off at twelve."

"All right. I'll take care of the kid, too. Is this H you brought?"

"Yeah—you got plenty M haven't you?"

"I'll give you the office when I need some."

"I'm off Sunday."

"Better bring some in Saturday night."

"Right. I'll shove off now. Be back in an hour."

When the guard had gone Murphy repeated his performance with the spoon, giving a shot to Benny after he had taken his own dose. Benny sat on the bed as before, and he began to sweat. Soon he was wet all over, and he felt dizzy. He started to get up but thought it would be better to stay where he was. He was quite comfortable and everything seemed far away.

"What was—that?" he mumbled.

"Something to fix you up. You'll feel great. You'll sleep to-night."

"That last made me feel funny. I'm sweatin'."

"Sure, it was different. We take a bang of M an' a bang of H an' that's what we call a whiz-bang. It makes you feel up-to-date. It's the real McCoy."

"Give me some more. Le's see how it feels."

"You had plenty for the first time. I'll give you some more later. How you feel now?"

"Pretty good."

"You feel sleepy?"

"No; I just feel good. I feel like flyin'."

"I know how you feel."

"I feel like everything is all right."

"Sure; everything *is* all right."

Benny smoked another cigarette and sat on the bed without saying anything. The haze of the smoke looked very peaceful. He felt very peaceful all over. For a moment he tried to think about Lou Warren going away and about Fat Hall and Chick McTeague, but they seemed to all float away on the cigarette smoke. He leaned back against the wall, and Jew Murphy picked his cigarette off the bed when it slipped from his limp fingers.

IX

WHILE Benny, under the strange law that says the man who witnesses a crime may be locked up as a material witness no matter how utterly innocent he may be in fact, stayed in jail and became a drug addict, the people who were not in jail began to adjust themselves, according to their various natures, to life under Prohibition. Politicians who had always been cronies of the brewers, distillers and saloon keepers in their legal day clamped themselves onto the bootleg industry and began to wax fat. Bootleggers and speakeasy operators voted dry when newspapers held straw votes. The biggest bootleggers contributed to the funds of the various anti-liquor leagues and other organized meddlers in the nation's business. "Behold," cried the reformers in high glee, "the great American public favors Prohibition. See how the citizens vote for it and how they spend money to help enforce the law."

The bootleggers and the politicians laughed and hoped that the Eighteenth Amendment would stay on the books forever. It had created their business —a business of huge profits. As long as the nation was dry they would continue to roll in the gold, but once the licensed saloon came back nobody would patronize them any more. Bootleggers would have to seek other rackets, and politicians would lose an issue as well as a lucrative graft. Vote dry? Of course they'd vote dry. Every bootlegger in America was a Prohibitionist.

Every politician who controlled a speakeasy or who was paid juicy protection money by the underworld spoke up for the enforcement of the law. They knew damned well the law never could be enforced. The smoke screen was safe.

Then there were the drinkers. Thousands of them voted for dry candidates and gave the members of the zealous Anti-Saloon League the chance to blazon the apparent fact that the people wanted no more booze. Had these drinkers imagined for one minute that they would ever be deprived of their gin and whisky they would have crushed each other in the rush to vote wet. The farce was complete with the bootleggers, the crooked politicians and the hypocritical drinkers all raising their voices in harmony with the Anti-Saloon League in a mighty chorus of *Ave Volsteads.* Those who dared raise their voices against the graft were the honest brewers and distillers, and the drinkers who were ethical enough to want their drinks to come to them legally instead of from the underworld. But the reformers continued to claim that the bootleggers were fighting Prohibition, imagining that a man would bite the hand that is feeding him. . . .

August Wagner couldn't quite understand why Benny should remain in jail. Fat Hall was out and seemed in no hurry to go to trial. It did not seem right that Benny should suffer while the guilty man went free. He spoke to McTeague, but the politician assured him that he had nothing to worry about.

"Just take it easy and we'll fix things. We don't want to start anything that might stir up trouble. Your kid will get out all right. We got to leave him there a while so the D.A. won't get suspicious."

"But he ain't done nothing."

"I know it. That don't make any difference. Why, I know of one case where a whore clipped a sailor for his wallet. The sailor called the police, an' they took him in with the woman. She had all his money. She paid bail with it an' got out, but the sailor stayed in jail three months. Another time a woman witness stayed in jail sixteen months." *

"Well, Benny's been in ten months."

"You wanta start somethin' with the D.A. an' get a charge against him? They might send him to prison for ten years."

"Well, I think a good lawyer could do somethin'."

"You gotta keep on the good side o' the D.A. You don't wanta get him down on you."

"Ain't Hall never goin' to trial?"

"Pretty soon, I guess. Soon's he gets his business

* Vide *The Riddle of Society*, Chas. Platt, p. 188.

goin' good. Benny's all right. He's got plenty to
eat an' a good place to sleep. He ain't kickin', is
he? What you worried about?"

"I don't know. He ain't natural. I see him once
a month, an' he always seems in a hurry to get rid
of me. Acts nervous an' shy. Don't seem to care
about bein' there."

"Well, if he don't care he's all right, ain't he?"

"No," said August. "No, he ain't all right. It
ain't all right for a kid to be satisfied in jail. I don't
like it."

"Don't worry. Hall will go to trial soon, an'
soon's it's over they'll turn Benny loose."

A good lawyer could have got Benny out, but August had to listen to his masters. Who would be protected by politics must first become the slave of politicians.

Chick McTeague, under the *sub rosa* direction of
his father, had made a good thing of Wagner's place.
August continued to pose as owner, for Chick did
nothing so crude as to openly proclaim his manager-
ship of the joint. Ostensibly he was merely an employee, knowing nothing of the insides of the business. Wagner saw that Alderman McTeague knew
what he was about. At first he sighed about it a bit,
but he soon learned to appreciate the value of Chick's
advice: "Get all you can, and to hell with the law;
nobody really cares anyway."

Other changes had taken place in the neighborhood. Ten months after Benny went to jail, or

early in 1921, saw most of the district deserted by the respectable people. Because of its convenient location and its broad-minded and well-greased police captain the ward became the recognized underworld of the city. Restaurants and lunch-rooms became speakeasies, pool rooms had back rooms for gambling, and the larger houses became bordellos. Prohibition's new politicians, the bootleggers, had to have protection—and it's impossible to protect one form of crime without nourishing and protecting all the others. Alderman McTeague was on the payroll of seven small speakeasies, four bordellos and eleven gambling joints in addition to the income he derived from Wagner's.

The Government concentrated the bonded liquor supply into few warehouses, and the thefts from August's warehouse were discovered. McTeague had that fixed so that the guard went to jail. The guard pled guilty to neglect of duty, some one paid his fine, and the matter was dropped. McTeague grinned and made another contribution to the coffers of the Anti-Saloon League.

Chick McTeague added to his own glory. He had always been a leader in his class. The younger boys, and even some of the older ones, had followed him in childhood. As a leader in boyish games he had been unquestioned. Later, as the instigator of neighborhood forays, they had blindly followed him. Now, as a bootlegger, he was a big shot. His cronies all knew that he, and not August Wagner, was the

manager of the speakeasy. Few knew that his father
was the real director. They gave Chick credit for
having complete control. The magnitude of it rather
awed them. Many of them were still naïve enough
to believe that it took a daring man to defy the new
law.

Chick's one rival was Fat Hall. Ed Warren's old
barber shop had taken on a new vitality under the
hands of the fat man. Hall was a rum runner. The
stuff was landed at Lido Beach and trucked to the
city. The barber shop was the clearing house.
Strange trucks, without lights, slipped up in the night
and vanished before daylight. Silent, rapidly working men became active, and the patrolman on the
beat discovered that important business elsewhere
kept him from that block. An arc-light on the
corner sputtered one night and went out. Evidently
there was no complaint, for the city did not repair
it. Its light had been too revealing for the business
of the trucks and the barber shop.

Chick saw the fat man rising in power and he resented it. Hall, more reckless and brutal than Chick
or his friends, was one of the first of the big booze
racketeers who did not hesitate at murder and mayhem to gain his ends. His henchmen were thugs.
In the old days they would have been afraid to show
their faces in daylight for fear of arrest, but now
they had the protection accorded Prohibition's new
criminals. Hall was earning a reputation for himself outside of the underworld. His name appeared

in the newspapers, and reporters interviewed him after a particularly spectacular episode in bootlegging or rum-running. Everybody knew what he was doing, but there was no evidence on which to convict him. McTeague, too, protected him. McTeague was keeping his agreement. He had promised Hall protection in return for Hall's promise not to tell the truth when his trial should come up. And Mc-Teague needed Hall, for many of the speakeasies from which McTeague collected graft got their booze from the rum runner. The supply taken from August's warehouse had long since been exhausted.

But Chick saw no reason to keep on the good side of Hall. He hated him. The affair of the fifty gallons of whisky still rankled. He did not hesitate to let his dislike of the fat rum runner be known. He talked about Hall, and Hall knew it. Outwardly indifferent, inwardly Hall was a smoldering volcano waiting the time to erupt. His resentment fed on itself. Benny had humiliated him and put him in hospital. Benny was Chick's follower. He recognized the fact that Chick was Benny's leader. He imagined that Chick had been the instigator of Benny's attack with the bottle of catsup. Benny was in jail. Hall's anger was against Chick, and Chick was talking about him—knocking him and belittling him.

Hall had his friends. Some of Chick's old gang had gone to work for the fat man. The more vicious of them found a thrill in their adventures under him.

135

Others were watchfully waiting, on the fence between Chick and Hall. They sensed the conflict between the two, and they wanted to cast their lots with the stronger. They wanted to follow the biggest of the big shots. If Hall should completely dethrone Chick then Hall would gain not only prestige but followers.

The open break came one afternoon as Chick, with Spike Davis and two of the gang, was walking along the street toward the speakeasy. Fat Hall, wheezing along the sidewalk, his huge bulk spreading almost from the buildings to the curb, stopped insolently in front of the quartette. He did not budge, and they, unwilling to accept the humiliation of a detour to avoid him, halted and glared at him.

Hall ignored the other three and spoke directly to Chick, holding his cigar between flabby lips as he did so.

"I just wanna tip you off," he sneered. "You been shootin' off your mouth too damn much to suit me. I'd hate like hell to muss you up, but if you ain't careful what you say it'll be just too bad for you."

"What the hell's eatin' you?" growled Chick. He was a bit uneasy, but he had friends with him and nothing to fear. "You can't bluff me, Hall. I ain't takin' no orders from you. Get outta the way."

"You'll take this order from me, you damn punk. I'm givin' you a break. Get wise to yourself."

"Let us get by," Chick demanded.

"Get out in the street if you wanta get by."

"Oh, yeah? Well, I guess you'll let us by." Chick gave Hall a shove in the belly and the fat man grunted. He raised one huge paw and slammed it down on the top of Chick's derby hat. The hat smashed and was crushed down over Chick's ears. Hall made a side-swipe with his arm and sent Chick sprawling. Chick's friends just stood and looked on, and Hall walked calmly on down the street. When Chick got up and pried the hat from his ears he saw that several passers-by were laughing. He saw that the two gangsters were grinning. Only Spike was serious. That evening he saw the two gangsters going into the barber shop. Hall had scored a victory.

X

CHICK McTEAGUE became sulky. Friends found him brusque and suspicious, watching them when they talked and glaring at them when they smiled. His vanity had been wounded to the quick. He could not forget the experience on the street with Fat Hall making an exhibition of him. He believed that the whole gang was secretly laughing at him. He was suspiciously on the alert for open laughter. He would not brook derision in his presence. If they wanted to laugh at him, why, let them do it when he wasn't around. That wouldn't be so insulting. He'd show them that he wasn't kowtowing to anybody. To hell with them all. He could get along without them.

But Chick could not get along without them, and he knew it bitterly. He saw half a dozen of his old gang join forces with Hall. He could picture the fat monster laughing at him, gloating over his defeat. He could imagine Hall finally driving him out of the neighborhood entirely. Chick had always been the undisputed leader there, and he could not tolerate the thought of the power resting on another.

But Hall gained prestige with every new day. Chick saw that more of his old associates were becom-

138

ing friendly with his enemy, and he heard others who still pretended to be his friends voicing words in praise of the rum runner. The gang admitted that Chick was a big shot, but Hall was so much more spectacular. He awed them and appealed to their imaginations.

A week after the comedy on the street Chick sat at a table in the speakeasy talking with the arrogant bravado that had been growing on him of late. Old August was back of the bar, reading a letter from Lou Warren who had written to ask what ailed Benny. Benny hadn't written to her in six months, and she was worried. August was worried too, and puzzled. He sat shaking his head while his bartenders waited on a row of toughs who stood at the bar. At the tables were groups of men and a few girls talking quietly. Some one mentioned the name of Fat Hall. Chick, his awkward form slouched in a chair, his elbows resting on the table between a small whisky-glass and a bottle of gin, sniffed contemptuously at the praise of his enemy.

"That damn fat hog ain't so much," he snorted. "Some o' these days I'm gonna put him where he belongs."

Spike Davis, sitting opposite, spoke up warningly.

"Hell, Chick," he said, "you better not make cracks like that. Don't you know Hall's got pals around here?"

"What the hell do I care for the —— ——'s pals?

I ain't takin' nothin' from him or his louse friends."

Chick's voice had been raised. The joint became ominously still. Spike Davis and one or two of the others were a little scared. The place was full of dangerous characters. Some were friends of Hall's and some were his enemies. All were gunmen or knife wielders. Nobody very much relished the idea of getting mixed up in a row with that bunch. Chick had been drinking, and his ego had been suffering all week. He was ready to burst, and he wanted to talk about it. He didn't care who might hear.

"Let the damn louse come an' try to get me if he wants me," he shouted. "Damn him, he'll think he's standin' over that wop volcano—whatchu call it?—if he gets gay. Just let him start somethin'. It'll be just too bad for him."

It happened then. First a shot from the door, and then a voice—the voice of Hall himself—wheezing and labored, with gasping breaths between words so that he might have impressed an imaginative observer as resembling a bloated wild boar, exhausted and grunting hoarsely in rage.

"All—right—umahhh—then—I'll—umahhh—come an'—umanhh—*get*—umanhh—you—umanhh—you—umanhh—damned—umanhh—*punk*."

The last word was snapped out as he fired again. Chick slipped quickly to the floor and turned the table over for a shield. His own revolver began to spit, the bullets striking the wall on each side of Hall. The customers lined up at the bar stood nerv-

140

ously fingering their glasses. Chick fired again. Hall laughed. He was taking his time, letting Chick waste his ammunition. Hall was enjoying the situation, waiting his chance to plug Chick with one shot. It wasn't bravery that made him stand there under Chick's fire. It was egotism, his desire to hog the spotlight, to dramatize the moment. Chick didn't have a chance. His friends saw that. None tried to help him. It wasn't their fight. They all began to drop flat on the floor, trying to keep out of range of the bullets. Suddenly Chick raised his head and took careful aim at Hall. He fired. The huge body of Hall seemed to shake all over, like an immense bowl of jelly. He looked surprised. A red spot appeared on his chest. Suddenly he raised his heavy automatic and pumped five shots straight at Chick's exposed head. Chick gasped and clutched at his head. Blood trickled between his fingers. He toppled over.

Hall dropped his gun and walked over to a chair. He sat down heavily and looked around him, his eyes strangely wide. Then he grinned and slumped in the chair. His huge body seemed to roll to the floor like a ball. It quivered there for a moment and was still. One of the girls screamed. Her man slapped a rough hand across her mouth and snarled at her.

"Wanta give the bulls a rumble, you bitch? Le's get to hell outta here."

There was a scramble for the door. The underworld does not stay behind to identify its dead when the police are likely to be interested. Men knocked each other down in their attempt to get through the door first. A minute later only three persons remained in the speakeasy. Chick McTeague lay with his chin hung over one leg of the table, his face a mask of blood, dead. At the side of the room, where he had rolled from the chair, lay a greasy mass of dead flesh that had been Fat Hall. Over behind the bar old August Wagner sat on the floor with his back against the wall. In his hand was the letter from Lou Warren, a pitiful letter that asked why her sweetheart had forgotten her. He was clutching the letter tightly in his hand, but in his head was the bullet that had missed Chick McTeague. He wouldn't have to worry about answering the letter. . . .

XI

BENNY wasn't waiting any more. During the first few months of his jail life he had waited day by day for the welcome call to pack up and get out. Now he had ceased to wait in jail; he lived in jail, and his mind was on but one thing.

Jew Murphy's six-month sentence had been up long ago. Benny had found it necessary to look out for himself. For a while he depended on the few dollars he could beg from his father, but at most this would buy but a small bindle of stuff each week. After a few weeks he found that one shot a day wasn't enough. He had to have more, and necessity breeds invention. He learned how to make beaded bags which he sold for twenty dollars each. The materials for each bag cost five dollars, and it took him a week to make one. He worked all day and ruined his eyes. His back ached and he had pains in his chest. Sometimes his head would throb like the beating of an over-active heart, and he would have to blink his eyes rapidly to chase away the haze that half blinded them. It was hard work, this making of beaded bags in the poor light of the jail. Sometimes he would get a bag half done only to find that it was all wrong. It was heartbreaking to have to do it all over again, wasting the work of three or four days. He worked like a slave, but the fifteen dollars a week profit was enough to feed his habit.

Bill Jensen took the money each week and brought in the small bindles of heroin and cocaine. He brought only a few grains at a time, for he was afraid the warden would get wise sometime and frisk Benny. He didn't want any of the stuff found.

Benny liked heroin and cocaine better than morphine because they exhilarated him and made him feel good. Cocaine made him happy. At night, in his cell, he would sing loudly. The other men booed him and told him to shut up, but they couldn't quell his exuberant spirits when he was "charged."

Benny was glad that Jew Murphy had left the needle with him. He didn't want to use a safety pin and medicine dropper like he'd seen others do. They'd prick the flesh with the safety pin, then force the point of the medicine dropper into the incision, pumping the drug into the flesh. One man had taken his shots that way in the leg. His leg had swelled up and turned black and green. He went to the hospital and had it cut off. The doctor said he must have scratched his leg someway with a rusty nail.

After eight months in jail the inmates had given Benny a nickname. They called him Cokey Ben. The name stuck, and even the guards called him by it. Benny began to be proud of it. Nobody remembered that he hadn't been a "junky" when he

144

first came in. He was a junky now, and they treated him as an old-timer. He was quite gay about it when he felt good. Most of the time he forgot his troubles. Sometimes he thought of Lou and how he hadn't answered her letters. When he thought of her in that way he would go to his cell and cry and tell himself that he'd write to her that night. But he never did. He always forgot before night. When she finally gave up and stopped writing to him he didn't notice right away. Then one day he thought of her and began to cry and scold himself for not writing. Suddenly he remembered that he hadn't heard from her lately. To make sure, he got up and looked through his letters. Her last bore a date two months old.

'Jus' another damn woman,' he thought bitterly. 'Kid a gee along an' then give him the run-around when he gets in a jam. An' she said she loved me. Hell. Love! That's funny . . . funny . . . funny . . . To hell with love.'

He often wished that the old man would stop coming to see him every month. He had to hide his habit from the old man, and that was hard. He thought everybody could see what he was doing. He thought the old man could tell just by looking at him through the screen. When the old man came he had to lower his eyes and not talk much. Damn the old man anyway. Shouldn't come snooping that way. He began to hate his father because he was ashamed to let August know about his habit.

His fear of himself made him hate his father. He
was afraid of everybody. He didn't want people to
know things. People talked about him and laughed
at him behind his back. He was sure they did. He
didn't have any friends. Everybody was against
him. They thought he was no good.

When he got to thinking that way he became de-
pressed and cynical. He saw nothing good in anybody. For a few days at a time he would become
confidential with some one prisoner. He would tell
all about his stepmother and Ethel. The two
women had always been a shadow in his life, but
now they loomed solidly in his stimulated imagination. He told how they had tried to run him away
from home. The cocaine in his system fed his
imagination, and he told how they had tried to kill
him. They had put poison in his coffee. That was
a terrible thing for a mother and sister to try to do,
so he told it again and again. He began to call
Angela his mother and Ethel his sister. His old
lady and his sister had first tried to run him out, then
they'd tried to kill him. That was terrible. It was
worse for your old lady to do it than it was for a
step-mother to do it. People expected meanness
from a stepmother, but they expected a mother to
love her kids. His old lady and his sister hadn't
been natural. They'd tried to poison him. He told
it so often that he believed it himself. That made
him feel sorry for himself, and he cried. He seemed
to cry a lot. He thought:

'I ain't never had nobody to love me. Everybody wants to make a chump outta me. Damn 'em all. I ain't no baby.'

A chump. That was another idea that planted itself firmly in his drugged mind. He would suddenly turn against those who had been most friendly toward him. He would drop them, and wouldn't even speak to them. If they asked him what was the matter they were told that nobody was going to make a chump of him.

But when he had just taken a bang of H he would feel like a bird in the tree tops in June, and you couldn't stop him from singing. Just like the birds he sang without thought, merely because he felt good and there was nothing to worry about. He sang all the old songs that Lou had sung, and he learned the new ones from new inmates. He even made some up for himself, but they didn't have much meaning. His blue eyes danced and sparkled, and his white teeth gleamed between his quivering lips as he sang with no trace of self-consciousness.

When he was like that everybody liked him. A man couldn't hate a blue-eyed little kid who sang songs and laughed while he worked on a beaded bag that was to be sold for the price of more laughs and songs. You couldn't hate him even when he grew suspicious and spit at you when you tried to talk to him. In that case you just felt sad. You wanted him to be your friend. You rather loved him, and it hurt you to lose him. Usually he came out of it

147

in a day or two and apologized. When that happened you were relieved, and you smiled and for-
gave him. Cokey Ben had a winning personality.
He looked helpless and appealing, and you wanted
to help him. We always love those who appeal to
our strength.

Jew Murphy came to see him once or twice.
Murphy had promised Benny a good job outside. A
job working for him. Benny would be what is called
a pusher. He would sell bindles of junk to other
junkys, and he would make lots of money. Murphy
wanted to hang onto Benny. He thought Cokey
Ben would make a fine pusher. The cops wouldn't
know about him at first, and he'd get by. Also, the
time in jail would teach something to Cokey Ben.
He'd learn about how to tell a right gee from a
louse, and how to treat the junkys. Murphy thought
that every punk who wanted to be a racket gee should
go to jail for a year just to learn about rackets and
to get the feel of the underworld. Being with racket
gees in jail would make a kid loyal to his class. He'd
learn that he had to stick to the underworld and
never tell the cops anything. He'd learn that the
right gees know how to treat a guy, and he'd learn
that society was his enemy. He'd come out knowing
that he belonged to a class of he-men who would
stick by him all the time. He'd know that loyalty
to the mob was just like what the officers in the army
called patriotism. They told you that you were
Americans and that the best thing in the world was

to never betray your country even if you had to die
for it or kill for it. Loyalty to the mob was the
same thing. In jail a gee would learn that it was
right to stick faithfully to your kind.

Of course, it would be even better to learn all this
in a Big House—that would give you a record.
Once a gee had been in stir he was tagged. Never
good for much in a real racket.

Well, Jew Murphy was right. Benny was learning a lot. He'd go out and show them all what he
could do. He'd be a good pusher. Make a lot of
sugar.

Benny had learned a great deal of underworld
slang in his ten months of jail. He could talk just
like an old-timer now. Chick McTeague and the
gang would be surprised.

Benny began to think of Chick McTeague and
Fat Hall. He didn't worry about them any more.
He knew something now that they didn't know. He
was a junky, and he was going into a real racket.
Bootlegging was all right, but selling junk was better.
He'd not have to take orders from Chick or anybody.

The door opened and the deputy stuck his head in.

"Wagner," he called, "pack up. You're goin'
home."

"Gee," said Benny, "they must have turned Fat
Hall out."

"No," said the deputy, "they didn't turn him out.
He got bumped off last night. There won't be any
trial."

"Well," said Benny, "I'm glad of it."

"Your friend Chick McTeague got his, too."

"Yeah? Ain't that something!"

"And, Cokey Ben, I hate to say it—gosh, I don't know how to tell you—but your old man—he's—he's—*bumped off* too."

"Well," said Cokey Ben, "I'm gettin' out o' the can anyway. Yeah, they can't keep me no longer. Ain't that something!"

PART THREE

I

LOUELLA WARREN finished her song in that sobbing, vibrant voice that had won fame for her among the night-club habitués of Broadway and among the radio fans. When Louella finished a number there was always a moment of silence before the shouting and applause began. She seemed to leave her hearers in a sort of trance, and they had to snap out of it before they could become noisy again. Walter Winchell said in his column that she was a female Rudy Vallée, and it was pretty generally conceded that should Louella and Rudy ever appear together singing duets, the perfect night-club team would have been found. And what a sensation if Al Jolson should write their song for them, a song for a man and a woman parting forever, sobbing their last good-bys, crooning their heartbreak. That was the sort of thing Louella did, and the public liked it and asked for more.

Louella had written the sentimental sobbing song, "I'll Still Be Your Pal If You Need Me." Always when she sang it she looked out over her audience, seeming to be searching for some one beyond things seen. Sometimes people wondered to whom she was singing that song; surely the intense feeling she exuded in the words could not all be acting. But Louella never told them anything. She never told any one that she had written the song to a lover she'd never forgotten.

All these years, and she hadn't forgotten. Often, alone in her dressing room, she would go back over the years in New York, wondering how things had come about as they had.

Success? Well, people called this success. She had dreamed of bigger things, true, but it was a fact that everybody couldn't sing in opera. There was still a chance. She'd seen other cabaret girls picked from the chorus and elevated to the stage of the Metropolitan. Some of them didn't make as much money as she made at the Chez Carlo. Prohibition had destroyed the old-time cabarets and the old-time quiet restaurants with music and concert singing. Time was when full-throated divas sang arias during dinner, and orchestras played subdued waltzes while quiet waiters served delicious dishes to epicures. The night-clubs had done away with that. People wanted jazz and gin, not refined music and good food. Night-clubs had to supply "hostesses" for the visiting yokels. Respectable people, too, went to the night-clubs and mingled with the racketeers and ladies of the evening. People were no longer discriminating in their choice of associates. The Chez Carlo was like other night-clubs—a glorified speakeasy.

In the old days, when Lou Warren dreamed of a

career, she would have been insulted had any one offered her a job in a house of assignment entertaining the clients with popular songs. Now it was quite proper. Prohibition had created new values, new standards of ethics.

Still, she didn't want to do this sort of thing all her life. She had her dreams, and some day she'd achieve them.

As she finished singing "I'll Still Be Your Pal If You Need Me" she smiled at her audience and walked slowly over to a table near the illuminated fountain in the center of the room. Two women were alone at the table, and all through her song Louella Warren had watched them, fearful lest they should get away.

As Louella approached, the older of the two women looked up at her, then dropped her eyes in a startled, apprehensive manner. The younger woman went on picking at her lobster, a petulant expression of boredom on her somewhat hardened face. She was dressed in a rather dowdy evening gown of blue sequins, and her bobbed hair had that dirty appearance of hair that has been bleached once and then neglected. She did not look up until Louella Warren rested her knuckles on the edge of the table and said:

"Isn't this Mrs. Wagner—and Ethel?"

"I was Angela Wagner at home," replied the older woman. "I'm Angela Chester now."

She seemed strangely proud of the distinction, and

Louella sensed that the woman had in some way been defeated, that she was struggling desperately to salvage something from life. The woman bore the expression of a beaten dog, not knowing whether to growl futilely or wag its tail in conciliation.

"I use the name of my first husband again," explained Angela.

"Is your husband—?"

"Dead," said Angela laconically, without emotion.

"Oh, I'm sorry."

"You needn't be."

"Who *are* you?" Ethel suddenly demanded, pausing a moment with a morsel of lobster on her fork.

"You don't remember—Lou Warren?"

"Lou Warren—oh, the barber's daugh— Oh, Lou Warren!"

"I've changed," Lou admitted. "I suppose I was rather plain and uninteresting when I left home eight years ago. But I knew you at once—the two of you. I had to speak to you."

"Oh, I'm glad—glad you did," Angela said, a little catch in her voice.

'She's been lonely,' thought Lou. 'She's had a rough time of it some way. She's glad to see some one she knows.'

"I wanted to ask you about things at home," Lou went on. "You see, I haven't heard anything in over seven—years."

"Where's your mother?" Angela asked.

"Married again—and gone off somewhere. I

don't know where. I've never seen my father since
that day he sold the shop and went away. Mother
divorced him."

"Don't ask questions, mother," Ethel said prig-
gishly, cracking a claw of the lobster. "I imagine
she doesn't like to discuss personal affairs."

"Oh, that doesn't matter. It doesn't matter in the
least. I'm not proud, you know. One can't be."

"Well, *I* am," said Ethel.

"Hush," said her mother. "Ethel, you're being
unpleasant."

"Oh, hell, mother. You can't nag now. Go
ahead and gossip. I'll eat my lobster."

Angela sighed.

'That girl has been a trial to her,' thought Lou.
'The poor woman is distracted. Ethel is treating her
now like she treated Benny.'

"I wanted to ask you about Benny," she said.

"What about him?"

"What is he doing? Where is he?"

"I don't know."

"We're not interested in him," said Ethel grat-
ingly. "And, mother, you *do* know where he is and
what he's doing. Why don't you tell her?"

"Ethel!"

"Oh, hell. Have it your own way then. There's
no use hiding things though. Let her know the
truth."

"What is it?" Lou asked, worried.

"Oh, nothing."

157

"But there must be something. Tell me."

"There's nothing," Ethel repeated, then, incon-
sistently, "Let mother tell you."

"Benny's no good," said Angela.

"What is he doing? He never wrote after his
first two or three letters."

"He couldn't," said Angela.

"His father never answered my letter to him."

"August was shot to death with your letter in his
hand. He never had time to finish reading it, far
as I know."

"But Benny?" Lou was bewildered by the unconnected outbursts of the two women.

"Well, Benny Wagner is no good. He was a jail-
bird."

"Oh, I see. He went to jail. You hate him for
that?" Lou was greatly relieved.

'Of course,' she thought, 'they'd be like that.
They'd drive him to jail and then condemn him for
being there.'

"I knew he was in jail," she said. "But it wasn't
his fault. He was merely a witness."

"He's a dope fiend now," Ethel said brutally.
She busied herself with the lobster and did not look
into Lou's face. Angela sat back and looked her
consternation. She hadn't meant to bring it out so
unexpectedly.

"What do you mean? Tell me—quick." Lou
was pale.

"That's right," said Angela, plunging in desperately. "He uses dope. We had to chase him away when he came home. August was dead, and August left all his money to me. I didn't have to give Benny any, so I thought I'd better not—he'd buy dope with it."

"You drove him out—of his *home?*"

"He was a dope fiend."

"You sent him away without trying to help him?" Lou was trying to assemble the facts in her mind, trying to comprehend the enormity of what she had heard. Ethel placidly ate her lobster in the manner of a satisfied judge who has just condemned a felon to penal servitude, but Angela sat back in her chair with wide-open eyes, frightened and timid because of what she had done. Eight years under the domineering egoism of Ethel had sapped her of all independent personality. It was like Ethel to start something and then calmly go on eating lobster while her mother had to face the consequences. Lou was looking at her in a manner that seemed to demand justification, and suddenly Angela wished that she could offer some really terrible reason for turning Benny out. If only she could say that he had struck her, or tried to rob her, or even that he had been ungrateful for what she had done for him. But no —she had done nothing for him, and he had done nothing to her.

"He was a dope fiend, I tell you," she said doggedly, desperately wishing that Ethel would enter the breech and offer reasons more convincing. Oh,

Ethel could say just a few words and make Benny seem like a monster of iniquity. Ethel had said those few words to Angela, and Angela had turned him out that day when he came back from jail with the hypodermic syringe that had fallen from his pocket in the living room. Nothing to do then but turn him out. Ethel had said so, and Ethel had a way of saying things that brooked no argument. She was always getting her way with people, and people were always sorry afterwards that they had given in. Maybe that was why Ethel could never keep a man, why no man had ever asked her to marry him. But Ethel didn't care. Not she. She was sufficient unto herself. She scorned people, and people were afraid of her. But why couldn't she unbend once in a while? Why, if their treatment of Benny must be defended before Lou Warren, couldn't Ethel say something to help? Of course, she realized, Ethel didn't consider that she had any need for a defense. Benny was out, and out he should stay. They had a right—a legal right—to drive him out. Legal rights were the only rights worth observing.

"I wish you would tell me all about it, if you don't mind," Lou said. She was calm now, more calm than was Angela.

"Oh, he met somebody in jail, and whoever it was gave him dope. He used it every day. I heard all about it, a little at a time. He was crazy over what he saw that night when Hall killed the man with the meat cleaver. He dreamed about it. He had to take dope to make him forget—"

"No excuse at all," Ethel suddenly snapped, and Angela sighed like a toy balloon from which the air is being slowly let. She looked at Ethel hopelessly, then turned again to Lou, telling her the rest of the story without any hint of sympathy or excuse for Benny. But Lou had glimpsed, in those first few sentences, and in the emptying expression on Angela's face at the interjection of Ethel, the whole story of Angela's regret and unhappiness, and her subjection to the tyranny of Ethel.

While Angela told everything in little rushing torrents of cruel words interspersed with reticent pauses Lou looked at her through a mist. It seemed that a curtain hung between her and Angela. Between the curtain and her mind was the past with little Benny crying out for her love. Beyond the curtain was Angela, tearing at her heart, explaining, blaming Benny, justifying herself, giving birth to words that tore her with anguish because she feared Ethel and blamed herself and because she felt that she should have no reason to blame herself. Outside of everything sat Ethel eating lobster. It was maddening to see that dowdy girl holding herself cynically aloof while the universe was tumbling about them.

'She drove him out. She hated him. Hated him always, since they were children. Hate hate hate hate she'd done her work and she's satisfied but she's not happy happy she can't be happy. Two women hate each other Angela and Ethel hate each other have to live have to live with each other hate each other Ethel hates her mother Angela can't understand they hate each other and they have to live with each other and get on each other's nerves nerves kill each other slowly but Ethel is strong like a devil and can hate harder but they're being punished for Benny turning Benny out dear Benny out sweet little Benny my Benny dear dear sweet Benny love love love you turned you out now they're trapped with each other they'll suffer.'

"I must go back—go back and save him."

Ethel laughed.

"Save him—I should like to see you."

"I must. It's all my fault. I shouldn't have left him. I told him to make good for me. Oh, he must have been terribly despondent there in that filthy jail, brooding over the injustice of it. That fat hog Hall was out on bail all the time."

"That's the law," said Ethel.

"Oh, the law! The law! Why do people keep on talking about the law?"

"We have to obey it," said Ethel snootily.

"Don't talk to me about that," said Lou bitterly. "I've lived on Broadway for over six years. I've seen things."

"No doubt," Ethel half sneered.

"Law! You sit here drinking highballs and talking about law. This club is a speakeasy, and every one knows it. The police know it, and collect their share. Half of the patrons here are underworld racketeers, big ones who are above the law. It's a joke. That's why I can work here and bootleg whisky for a living. Oh, yes, that's what we hostesses do all right. We sing so people will come in and buy drinks, and we get a cut of the profits. But I don't care. Everybody's crooked, so why shouldn't I get my share?"

"She's been drinking," said Ethel.

"I have not. But I'm going to now." She opened the flask she had taken from her stocking and quickly swallowed half its contents. She had become a bit hysterical.

"Yes, I can drink as well as the rest if I need it. I need it now."

"Please," Angela said anxiously, "be careful."

"Oh, let her be," said Ethel. "She wants to be as bad as Benny."

"Oh, Benny! Angela, I'm sorry. I lost control for a moment. You can't understand, though."

"Oh, I do!" Angela exclaimed, almost inaudibly.

"I'm going back to him," Lou said decisively.

She didn't think of what she had to give up. She was making money here, and her name was a byword on Broadway, but she could give up everything and go back and devote her life to Benny.

'Oh, if only I'd known why he didn't write. I thought he'd forgotten me. I should have known better. Oh, what have I done?"

She was thinking of Carlo. . . .

'Oh, I'm guilty. I've wronged Benny. I've been unfaithful. Carlo . . . Carlo . . . Carlo. I don't love Carlo. I know it now. I thought I did, but I can't. I've never loved him. I'm glad he loved me. I made him happy because he loved me. He gave me everything but happiness and took everything from me but love. . . .'

Perhaps, after all, this was being faithful—giving her body to another but always reserving her heart for Benny. She had thought that he had forgotten her. Hadn't that given her the right to give herself elsewhere? She had never really loved Carlo—yes, she had too; at least she had thought she loved him. He had been so wonderful at first. She hadn't really known what passion was. When she left Benny she had been a child, now she was a woman capable of love. Perhaps Carlo had given her a greater capacity for loving Benny.

'He did wake me up,' she thought. 'It's been wonderful to be with him. I thought I'd always love him and be happy with him, but that was when I thought I'd lost Benny.'

There was no doubt in her mind but that she would go at once to Benny. She did not care that it would be hard to explain things to Carlo. She had something to do, and she'd do it. Carlo would suffer, but that was a side issue. He would have to look out for himself. She was going out of his life with no regrets.

All through the years she had thought of Benny as something lost, something to store away in memory. She had been certain she would never see him again. And Carlo had offered—well, what, after all, had he offered? Love? Yes, he loved her, but he was married and love would never really have a chance. He had loved her with his whole soul, and because of his deep understanding of her artistic nature, because of the beauty of his conception of love, his Latin chivalry combined with Broadway sentimentalism and gaudiness, she had sought refuge in his arms. She had been lonely. He had loved her. Benny had left her, and nothing mattered. It was good to find escape with some one who loved her. She was very fond of Carlo.

She remembered their first meetings. Carlo, with his Prohibition-born Chez Carlo, had ridden to wealth and fame on the crest of the wave of illicit liquor that had engulfed the nation. The saloon had disappeared from the land, and in its place had come the speakeasy and the night-club, and because the public supported twice as many of the new speak-easies as it had the old saloons, Carlo found business good. With ten small speakeasy joints operating in various parts of the city for the cheaper trade, such as laboring men and small-time crooks, he had soon acquired sufficient money to open the new and magnificent Chez Carlo, with its own fleet of rum boats operating from Canada and its own generously paid staff of police officers and officials who saw that no padlocks ever impeded the progress of the club.

Here it was that Lou Warren had found employment. Her voice, being really good, and her personality as a blues singer had put her over at once. She clicked with a wow, and Broadway paid tribute. With Benny in her thoughts she had written the song that sentiment-loving Main Stemmers cried for— "I'll Still Be Your Pal If You Need Me." At night when she sang it she saw only Benny, and the crowd loved her sobbing voice.

Carlo, who had become friendly with her at once, said to her:

"Baby, they take it big. The Main Stem is hard boiled and wild all right but it sure likes to cry. Sob at the suckers and they eat out of your hand. You got something, baby. You got art."

She never let him know that the sob in her voice came naturally when she thought of Benny. She became a part of Broadway. She became worldly-wise, but she never really became sophisticated.

And then—Carlo and love. Carlo telling her that he wanted her. Carlo smiling his boyish, impudent smile, showing his even white teeth. Carlo looking into her eyes with his caressing black-eyed gaze. Carlo holding her in his arms and whispering with his lips against her cheek. Carlo taking her to the new apartment and telling her that he really loved her.

'Oh, it's going to be hard on poor Carlo. I wish I didn't have to hurt him. But Benny . . .'

While Lou thought of the past Angela's hard, monotonous voice droned on, and Ethel finished her lobster and sat silently watching the dancers. Suddenly Carlo, sleek and polished in his professional manner, was smiling over them and hoping they were enjoying the evening. Angela was abashed into silence, and Ethel brightened and smiled encouragingly. Carlo rested a caressing hand on Lou's shoulder and said he would like to meet her friends. Lou introduced them, wondering vaguely for a moment why any one should desire an introduction to two unpleasant cats. But this was the professional Carlo, the Carlo of the Chez Carlo, the Carlo who had to flatter nonentities as well as celebrities.

"But such charming ladies should not be alone," he exclaimed. "Perhaps Miss Chester would care to dance?"

"Oh, I'd love to," Ethel gushed.

And so Carlo took her out on the floor, and the leader of the orchestra took his cue and cut the music very short, so that the dance lasted only a minute.

When they returned to the table Carlo looked strangely at Lou and asked her to dance. The orchestra got the signal to prolong the dance, and Carlo held Lou very tight and said:

"I'm going to lose you."

"Carlo, what do you mean?"—nervously.

167

"You're going to leave me. That Chester girl told me all about your little hop-head back home."

"Carlo!"

"It's all right, baby. She was catty, but I saw through her all right. She tried to make it look bad for you, but I saw how you looked and I knew. You love him, don't you?"

"Carlo—what must you think of me?"

"It's all right."

"I'll have to tell you about it, Carlo."

"It's all right, baby."

She told him about Benny, and about their early love and about their heartaches. She couldn't keep the sob from her voice, and he held her more tightly and whispered:

"I know now how you love him. I know what your singing that way meant. But I thought it was art."

"Oh, Carlo—you used to say I could sing for the suckers and get anything I wanted. Oh, Carlo, I hope—"

"No, Lou; I don't think you made a sucker of me. I understand you."

"Carlo, do you love me?"

"I always loved you. I love you more now because I see how you can love some one. I thought you loved only your art. You didn't love me, but I was satisfied because I thought you loved me as much as you could love a man. Lou, I think you're going to kill me."

168

"Carlo, don't talk that way. You make it difficult for me. You make me want to love you."

"If I wanted to make you love me now I could keep you. But I won't do that. No, baby, I won't do anything like that. I know how you feel. You feel like mothering me a little and nursing me because you think I'm hurt. When a woman feels that way a man can keep her always, but I won't do that. You must go to your little hop-head."

"Carlo, you do understand so much—"

"Lou, sometime you could have been a great singer. You would have gone on from this to musical comedy and then to opera. That was the way I expected to lose you. I never thought I could keep you. Now you'll go on back to your Benny and you'll never sing again. I know. You're going to have a hard time of it, but you'll feel good about it because you'll have Benny. Maybe you'll cure him."

"I want to, Carlo."

"You can always come back to me if things go wrong. That song you wrote to Benny—I'll sing it to myself."

"Carlo—"

"You'd better go to-morrow. I'll go over and dance with Miss Chester now, and you can go home and pack up. There's five thousand dollars in the wall safe. Take it. You'll need it, Lou, to cure your little hop-head. I won't see you again. Remember me, Lou."

. And so, without saying good-by to any one or even

letting the Main Stem know its crooning idol was not to sing it to tears any more, Louella Warren got her last glimpse of distant Broadway as she turned into the Grand Central Station. Behind her she was leaving a career, the goal of her dreams, but before her was Benny—and her love which had been first and which should be last.

COKEY BEN was in jail again. Cokey Ben had gone to jail quite regularly during the seven years. Sometimes he went to take a "cure" and sometimes they picked him up for possession of narcotics. Sometimes Jew Murphy got him out, but if Jew Murphy felt that Cokey Ben really needed a cure he left him there to do his bit. Cokey Ben was a good worker. He could sell more of the stuff than any other "pusher" on Jew Murphy's ample staff. Murphy often congratulated himself on the acquisition of Benny. He had done a good job the day he got Benny hooked. Benny had come out of jail and gone directly to work for him when he found that he wasn't welcome at home. It hadn't taken him long to get wise to his new racket. There were times of panic when drugs were hard to get, and at these times it didn't matter so much that Benny went to jail. Besides, what more convenient time for a cure than the times when junk was scarce anyway? They had it all doped out, and Benny was careful.

Whenever a big shipment of the stuff got safely in from Europe and landed in the hands of the big fellow for whom Jew Murphy worked, Murphy would give Benny the office:

"The pig is fat, Cokey. Watch your step."

Benny knew then that the supply of drugs was equal to the demand, and that he must steer clear of the law while the easy money was coming in. At such times the retail prices were slightly reduced, and customers bought as much as they had the ready money to pay for. But if a big shipment happened to be "knocked off" by the police—and even the almost perfect organization, of which Jew Murphy was second only to the big fellow who could not be named, could not always forestall such a blight— prices were boosted at once and a panic was on. At these times the addicts had to pay for the losses suffered by the organization. At such times Jew Murphy didn't mind letting Benny stay in jail. It was best for Benny to take a cure now and then. It kept him interested. But if an extra big shipment got through while Benny was locked up Jew Murphy would send some one over to whisper to him, "The pig is fat," and something would be done at City Hall and Benny would be back on the street. Benny was always too wise to inquire into the workings of City Hall in these matters. If he suspected that a certain alderman named McTeague was the influence behind his sudden liberations he said nothing. It was certain that the alderman never did anything in person. It was also certain that the alderman owned a magnificent estate in an expensive suburb, and that his motor cars and yachts had no rivals in the matter of size and gaudy trappings. And Benny knew, of course, that Jew Murphy's headquarters was a somewhat dowdy night-club located in the building that had once been his father's saloon, and he knew that some one had paid over a neat roll of cash to his stepmother when she sold the place.

Jew Murphy was a big shot, and he was the trusted lieutenant of the "Main Works." No other member of the ring was supposed to know who the Main Works was. Nobody could ever prove anything on the big fellow if exposure came. His name never entered a transaction. But Benny was not dumb. He knew. You couldn't have dragged the name from him with truck horses, but he knew. And because he could be trusted Jew Murphy had made him his own lieutenant. The organization was almost military in this matter of rank and power. There was the big fellow, the Main Works as they called him, who was the commander-in-chief, and there was Jew Murphy who was his confidant, and under Jew Murphy was Benny Wagner who knew all the pushers and acted as distributor to them. And Benny knew all the junkies, and he sold the stuff to them on the streets. The common "pushers" were the privates in the sinister army, and their ammunition was white powder and cubes of morphine. Just as Jew Murphy had captured Benny so Cokey Ben was capturing others, and these others in their turn were bringing new victims into the not-life of the captives of "junk." And because there was much money in small quantities of the stuff they dealt in, and because

173

where there is much money there is much protection and much corruption and graft, the crooked politicians waxed fat and the Government spent millions upon millions of dollars every year on Prohibition which most of the people didn't want, and most of the people forgot all about the narcotic traffic, which even the junkies wanted abolished. Benny used to laugh about that.

"Ain't that somethin'!" he'd exclaim when he read of a new series of raids by the dry agents. "Ain't that somethin', now! I was standin' in front o' this joint pushin' out M an' C to the trade, when up comes this machine with the Prohis in it. They crashed into the joint an' come out with two cases o' beer. While they was loadin' the beer into their car the manager o' the joint comes out an' grabs me. 'Hurry up,' he says, 'an' give me a sniff o' coke. I gotta go to court, an' I can't go down cellar an' take a drink o' booze while these guys is here. I gotta have somethin' to settle my nerves while I'm waiting for bail.'"

Cokey Ben, telling of this episode, laughed and went on:

"The guy was sellin' beer, understand? He was sellin' beer in his restaurant. They put a padlock on the joint for a few days, an' I made four new customers. Sure, I just stood by the door an' watched. When one o' his old customers come along an' seen the joint was knocked over I just give him the wink an' told him I knew of a better joint. Then I'd

174

spring it on him that I had better dope than the beer, an' not so much chance o' gettin' knocked off. A little bit would give him more kick than a case o' beer or a quart o' Scotch. Yeah, I made four new regular customers outta those Prohis raidin' that beer joint."

But now Cokey was doing another six-month stretch in the Pen. Cokey usually drew three months, but sometimes he had to take six. He didn't mind it much anymore. The thrill of starting a new habit was worth the suffering of kicking the old one. When he went to jail he made beaded bags and sold them at a small profit.

What did a little bit in the Pen matter anyway? He could take it easy and get through all right. Always had, hadn't he? Well, why put up a squawk? He'd get out again and hit up the old schmeck and everything would be jake. Good old schmeck! Made a gee feel like a million dollars. 'Course, he could get it here in the Pen if he wanted it, but it was better to wait. More of a kick. Long ago he had discovered that it didn't pay to monkey with the stuff in jail. Sometimes you couldn't get all you wanted, and when you were on the habit and couldn't get the stuff you pulled a tough bit. Better to go without until you hit the street. Then what a bang! The real McCoy . . .

The jailers all knew him now. He'd been in so often he seemed like one of the family. When he entered the front door in custody of a cop the keepers all went around telling the inmates, "Cokey Ben is back." They all called him Cokey and brought candy in for him, and sometimes a piece of cake or pie from the officers' dining room. Funny how a junky always craved sweets. Had a yen for it almost like the yen for schmeck. He'd eat candy and work on a beaded bag and sing songs until the lights went out and it was time to become quiet. He had no inhibitions whatever. He shouted out his songs, and if anybody beefed about the noise Cokey would just laugh, call the complainer an obscene name, and sing louder. He had no fear of anybody. He was small, but he knew how to use his knee on a man so that an adversary doubled up with pain and was helpless. He had no scruples about deforming any one who got in his way. Nor had he any other form of moral scruples. Cokey Ben was totally unmoral—amoral. Seven years of cocaine and heroin and morphine don't leave a man many barriers to total degeneracy. But Benny had a system of ethics. He was true to the underworld—he was a right guy. And he would die for a friend, if he really believed the friend deserved it. He had a sense of humor, and he never took people too seriously. He seemed to tolerate them rather than accept them. He'd often laugh at their troubles, but he'd often cry over his own. The Cokey Ben of 1928 was no older in appearance than had been Benny Wagner of 1919. He was still a child, a very hard-boiled and stunted child.

But he was full of life and gayety, and most peo-

ple who met him came under his spell and loved
him.   There wasn't a junky in the city who didn't
swear by him and want him as a pal, and there wasn't
a cop who didn't hate to pick him up and who didn't
look the other way sometimes when he came in sight.

He was making a woman's purse, weaving into it
one of the designs he had worked out for himself.
He would string the colored beads on the needle,
then work them into the mesh of the growing purse.
Before stringing the next row of beads on the loom
he would study the carefully drawn design which lay
beside him on a small table, counting the colored dots
on the paper and stringing the beads to match them.
His blue eyes were shifty, but they were sparkling
with good nature and he could keep them steady
when his attention was fixed on something.   He was
never quiet.   As he worked he sang the songs he'd
learned in jail.

He strung another row of beads and started another song, shouting it at the top of his voice:

"If I was a millionair and had lots of coin
    I'd buy a big plantation, I'd grow heroin;
    Piedmonts and Meccas I'd have growing on trees;
    In a house built of M where I could jab at ease,
    I'd have forty thousand layouts all inlaid with pearl
    So every hop-head that I know could bring along his girl,
    And each one with a habit would come leaping like a rabbit
            Down to that Cokeys' Jubilee."

When Benny came to the chorus he changed his
voice a bit, so that his singing was somewhat in the

177

manner of the lugubrious vaudeville tenors who try
to dramatize their songs, half singing and half talking them.   He raised his voice and shouted:

"Down to that Cokeys' Jubilee.
 Down on the isles of H, M and C;
 H is for heroin and M is for morph,
 C is for cocain to blow you head off.
 With autos and airships and nice sirloin steaks
 And every coke fiend there with his own private lakes—
 I'd dance the tango in the air, I'd live just like a millionair,
      Down at that Cokeys' Jubilee."

As Cokey finished the song he looked up and saw
his friend Jack, a trusty, standing in front of his cell.

"You sure make plenty noise," said Jack.   "Sound
like you're all charged up with H."

"No," said Benny, "I ain't on it now."

"Feelin' pretty good, hunh?"

"Up to date."

"Well, that's good.   Take it nice an' easy an'
you'll pull it O.K."

"Sure," said Benny, "I'll pull it.   I always do."

"Makin' another bag, hunh?"

"Yeah, I got to keep busy, Jack."

"You're a short-timer now, hunh?"

" 'Nother month."

"Well, you're lucky.   You got a break.   Me, I
got plenty time."

"Yeah?   How many years, Jack?"

"Five more months."

"Well, ain't that somethin'! You gotta lotta time, you have . . ."

"I wanta get home to the family, Cokey."

"Yeah . . . family. . . . Say, did I ever tell you about the time I met the junky broad on Market Street an' she took me home to her family?"

"No," said Jack. "No, you ain't told me that one."

"The cat was a junky," said Cokey.

"That don't make sense," said Jack.

"All right. 'Course you gotta butt in. I was gonna tell you about it an' you butted in. When I tell somethin' I gotta keep my mind on it."

"Go ahead an' tell it," said Jack. "I won't interrupt again. I just said it didn't make sense when you said the cat was a junky. I hadn't heard nothin' about no cat. Go ahead."

"No use tryin' to tell anything to you. You always butt in. I gotta tell things my own way, an' I get off the track when you butt in."

"Go ahead an' tell it," Jack repeated.

"You go to hell. Think I'm a chump."

"Aw, Cokey, don't act that way. What's wrong with you?"

"Nothin'."

"What about the cat?"

"I don't know any cats."

Benny returned to his work and Jack regarded him a moment with a grieved expression. He couldn't quite understand this unreasonable little junky who

179

could be so friendly at one moment and so hostile the next. He liked Benny, and he wanted Benny to like him consistently. At last Benny laid his work aside and said:

"I was pushin' junk on Market Street when this dizzy broad sides up an' cracks about H. I had her pegged all right. She was a schmecker an' no mistake. So I sold her the stuff. After that she met me regular, takin' the stuff every day.

"After while we got to be pretty good friends, an' we went out to parties a coupla times. Then she run outta dough. She'd been buyin' enough stuff for three ordinary junkies, so I figured maybe I wouldn't lose anything if I let her have a little on tick. I gave her a little for a while until I seen she wasn't gettin' any more sugar. Then she asked me to her house.

"Well, there was her old lady an' her old man, an' there was her old grandmother. This dizzy broad introduced me all around, then she asks me to break out the works. 'What,' I says, 'right here with your old lady and your old man an' your old grandmother?' She says, 'Bring it out an' cook up a bang. I don't give a damn if the pope and the twelve postals is here.' So I cooked up a bang an' she took it an' what you think she done? She walked right over to the old grandmother an' took the old hag's arm an' jabbed the stuff in, an' the old woman begins to laugh an' sing like a lunatic. 'She ain't had a shot for three days,' the broad says, 'an' it makes her happy.' I'll say it did!

"So then she told me to cook another bang, an' I did. This time she took it over to her old lady an' jabbed it in her arm. The old lady kissed her an' wanted to kiss me, but I was too quick for her. 'What the hell kinda family is this?' I said to myself. But it wasn't over yet. She gave the next shot to the old man, an' then she took one for herself. By that time I was beginnin' to think I was seein' things, an' my own yen was comin' on. I had just enough H left for one good bang for myself. I cooked it an' got all ready to shoot it when the broad grabbed it outta my hand an' said: 'Here, we can't forget Ignatz. We gotta give Ignatz his shot. Poor Ignatz ain't had a bang in three days. Where is Ignatz?' she asks the old lady. 'Under the stove,' says the old lady. 'He's been there sufferin' for two days.'

" 'What the hell,' I thought. 'Is this a bughouse? Ignatz must be a kid, but what's he doin' under the stove?' Well, I'd heard of young kids usin' it, so I thought I might as well go without my bang an' let the brat have it. The broad goes in the kitchen, an' pretty soon she comes back with Ignatz, an' Ignatz— what you think of this?—Ignatz was a cat! Yeah, Ignatz was a cat. An' the broad give him a bang o' H, an' Ignatz jumped around the room an' pretty soon he run out in the yard an' chased two bulldogs up a tree. Yeah, I seen that with my own eyes. He chased 'em right up the tree. An' I says, 'Well, ain't this somethin'!'"

"Yeah," said Jack, "it sure was some cat all right."

"An' there was me without a bang for myself, an' the damned junky cat leapin' all over the back yard chasin' the bulldogs up the tree."

"What kinda tree was it?" Jack inquired.

"It was just a tree, I guess. Maybe it was an apple tree. Yeah, I guess it was an apple tree."

"An' them bulldogs—where did they come from, hunh?"

"Well, how do I know? They was just there. Bulldogs always come from some place."

"Maybe they was junkies too," said Jack.

"Maybe."

"A junky cat!" Jack began to laugh, and his laugh grew until he almost lost his balance with mirth. Cokey Ben laughed too, and when Jack had subsided a bit he said:

"You gotta kick outta that, hunh, Jack?"

"Oh, lord! A junky cat an' bulldogs up a tree! Ho ho!"

"Yeah," said Benny, "I seen lots o' funny things. You'd be surprised. I'll tell you some more sometime. I see funny things in my racket."

"I guess you do," Jack agreed. "Yeah, your racket makes you see things all right."

"I had a parrot once," said Benny, "an' the parrot was a junky. He used to—"

"Benny Wagner out for a visit," called the keeper from the gate.

"Gee," said Benny, "I wonder who that is."

"I gotta go pull the brake," said Jack.

When the door opened Benny went out and found Lou Warren peering anxiously through the screen in the visiting room. He rubbed his eyes and looked doubtful, but he said:

"Well, ain't this somethin'!"

"Oh, Benny," she said, "I came back to you."

"Well," said Benny, "I'm here all right."

III

WHEN he got out she had the apartment all ready for him. She took no chances. She knew that Jew Murphy also would be waiting for Benny, and she was determined that never again should Benny fall into his clutches. She knew the day of Benny's release, and from daylight until ten o'clock in the forenoon when the gate opened and he emerged she waited with a taxi in front of the prison. She was glad that Jew Murphy had sent no one to meet Benny. She was glad that Murphy felt so sure of Benny that he believed he could sit back and wait for Benny to come to him. And she was glad that Benny had been in prison long enough to break his latest habit. She wouldn't have to go through the long, heartbreaking ordeal of curing him. He had promised her faithfully that he would use no more of the stuff, and she hoped that he would keep his word.

'If only I can keep him from thinking about it,' she thought, 'we can be happy. If he thinks too much about it he may go back in spite of me. But he loves me . . .'

She'd never forget that first meeting with him when she came back from New York and found him in the prison—the County Pen. He'd been suspicious and cynical and she'd had to convince him that she was sincere. He hadn't believed it the first day. He'd sent her away coldly, seemingly indifferent to her tears. He'd been very stubborn.

"You can't play *me* for a chump," he said, and that hurt her. But she understood his feelings. Eight years in New York among the night-club element had taught her a few things about the mental processes of addicts. She'd seen them fighting with their best friends and breaking the hearts of their lovers. She'd heard about them from the Broadway crowd. She hadn't taken any of it seriously because it hadn't come close to her, but she remembered. Now that she was to live through eternity with a junky she tried to recall all she had heard about them and their ways.

She didn't resent his attitude. She knew that she'd have to wait patiently until he came around, and that eventually he'd be all right with her. When he refused her visits she wrote daily letters to him, and she knew that he destroyed the first of them unread. She was afraid that none of them at all had been read, but when he finally gave in to her with tears in his eyes one day when he consented to see her and she pleaded with him through the screen, he confessed that he had read the later letters and cried over them.

"I read your scratches, kid, an' they made me cry. I don't know why I wouldn't give in. I wanted you, kid, but I just couldn't admit it. At night in bed I cried about you. I was miserable, an' for some reason I wouldn't give in. I just let myself suffer. I love you, kid. I'll always love you. I musta been crazy to treat you that way. God, what if I'd lost you . . ."

"You'll never lose me," she answered. "No, Benny, I love you and nothing can ever change that."

"I know it, kid. I can't ever forget that day you came to the old County Jail an' told me good-by. 'Member? We kissed each other through the screen an' you got black on your face."

"I remember, Benny. I remember everything."

They laughed a little then, and Benny said:

"Just wait till I get out. We'll fix up a swell little apartment together. We'll be happy, kid. I know we will. We'll get along up-to-date."

"And you'll never go back to junk?" Lou had learned to call the drug by its underworld name.

"Never, kid. If I used that I couldn't love you like I ought to."

"Oh, Benny, I'm so glad. It nearly killed me when I found out what you were doing."

"That's all over now, kid. We'll get married an' be happy."

And so they came together once more, and planned for the future. And Lou rented the apartment and bought little things to make it comfortable, and she was very happy about the building of her love-nest.

She had the five thousand dollars Carlo had given

her. She hadn't hesitated about taking the money. She knew that he honestly wanted her to have it and that he could afford to give it to her. She knew that she would need it. Without money she would have too great an obstacle to overcome. Benny would have less chance to recuperate normally. As it was, Benny wouldn't have to worry about money for a while. There'd be no need for him to go back to his racket to make a living. They could live a long time on five thousand dollars.

Benny liked the apartment.

"It's the money, kid," he approved. "It's got everything. We'll get along swell here."

There was one thing, she thought, that she must change in Benny; he'd have to learn better English.

'I wonder how I can go about it,' she thought. 'If I say anything he might be hurt. He's so sensitive. I must be careful with him. I wish I could read his mind.'

Reading Benny's mind would have been much like reading Chinese characters from top to bottom of the page, left to right, in the occidental manner. Benny's mind didn't run in grooves. It jumped about, first trusting and then suspecting every move of every one he knew. He watched, and he enlarged every action and imagined motives that had no existence. He imagined that everything had a meaning, and that every action was motivated. Everybody, he thought, sought gain. The world was divided into two camps —the chumps and the wise guys. Always he had a

fear of being a chump. He imagined that every one
was trying to do him. He looked with suspicion on
any one who made suggestions or offers of friendship. As in all things, he was inconsistent in this,
for he would become friendly with people who
meant him no good whatever, and while he remained
friendly he would defend such persons against all
attacks. In his life he had more than once been
astonished to discover that a trusted "big shot" was
really a "louse."

Lou sensed his condition and knew that it would
take very little to arouse his suspicion of her. She'd
had a sample of his peculiar twist during those first
days of her return from New York. She didn't want
him ever to turn from her that way again.

He was always telling her about those who had
tried to put something over on him. On the street
he pointed out old friends and warned her against
them.   •

"There's that louse Red Purvis," he said one day.
"The damn dog oughta be cooked."

"Who is he, Benny?"

"He's a racket gee. No good. Tries to make
himself out a good guy, but I'm wise to him."

"What did he do to you, Benny?"

"He ain't any good, that's all."

Benny didn't need reasons for denouncing a person. His drug-warped mind said to him, 'See that
guy Red Purvis over there? He's talking about *you*.
He's a louse. See how he looks at you. Remember

that time in Chi when he got dropped? Well, why do you think he got off with two years when his partner got five? Why, sure, he turned up his partner.' And Benny believed it for a while, just as he believed things of all his friends. He couldn't separate reality from phantasy. He didn't lie when he told about the family with the junky cat. He really had seen a family in which every member used junk, and the family really had a cat. At the time Benny had thought, 'Wonder what the cat would do if I gave it a bang?' And so he had let his imagination run on, and in time he began to remember the cat as a junky, and the bulldogs up a tree just naturally placed themselves on the scene to fill out the yarn. It was all true to Benny.

A few days later Red Purvis spoke to him on the street and he replied affably.

"Red's a good guy," he said.

He told Lou of the things he'd done during the eight years. Lou listened, and wondered if he expected her to believe everything. She laughed about the junky cat and about the parrot who knew all the popular songs and sang a complete repertoire every night for his daily supply of heroin.

"That parrot could sing everything," said Benny. "All I had to do was tell him what I wanted. He liked to sing 'Yes, Sir, That's My Baby' and 'Sundown.' He knew 'em all. He'd sing a dozen or so, then he'd yell out, 'Hey, Cokey, gimme my bang.'

That bird sure used up a lotta good junk. Used to eat coke, too."

"What did you do with him?" Lou inquired.

"I ate him," said Benny.

"Ate the parrot?"

"Yeah, I ate him. One night I came home from a party an' found him dead. He'd got into my stuff an' took an overdose o' M. Killed him dead. I looked at him there, an' I says to myself, 'Well, ain't this somethin'! Damn parrot's eat up all my morph an' I want a shot. What the hell! I'll eat the damn fool.' So I ate the parrot an' got a big kick out of him. He was all full o' junk. That was some roast, kid."

Benny and Lou didn't marry at once as they had planned. Somehow, it didn't seem necessary to either of them. They belonged to each other now as much as they would after marriage. They told each other that they were happy as they were. Lou admitted to herself that she was afraid, but she knew that she had never been more happy. She had Benny, and she would hold onto him. Someday he would adjust himself to life, and there would be no more cause for fear.

She wished, though, that he would forget about rackets and the underworld. His speech was charged with the esoteric argot of gangland, and his topics of conversation were mostly of things unlawful. He told of his past exploits, and he talked of his terms in jail and of his habits cured and recontracted.

When he spoke of jurk she caught the gleam in his eyes, and she saw that she had something to dread— a returning ghost that must be laid forever to rest before it could materialize into the thing of reality it had been while she was away. No, she couldn't let the white demon snatch him away from her again. She would fight and fight, and if need be she would kill him before it should take him again.

There were times when he was restless, and she found that taking him to the movies and cafés did not soothe him. He wanted more, and the realization of what he wanted terrified her. Now, she knew, if a bindle of heroin should be placed in his hands he would snatch it eagerly to him and fight her for its possession. He must not be allowed to see it. He must be distracted from the thought of it. Thinking of it would drive him on to a craving that he could not resist. He would break away from her and get it.

She loved him passionately, trying to make him forget the drugs in love. He loved her, but she sensed his incomplete satisfaction. Was this thing that he wanted stronger than love? She knew that it was the strongest thing in the life of an addict, but what about one who had been cured?

'There is no cure,' said the back of her mind, but she cried out in protest, 'There is—oh, there must be.' And yet—there was always the ghastly doubt.

"Benny—Benny—promise me you'll keep your word to me."

"I promised, kid. You know I promised."

"Benny, I'm afraid."

"Don't you think I love you, kid?"

"I know you do, Benny."

"I'll keep my promise, kid. If I broke it I couldn't love you."

They were in bed.

"Benny, why are you always glancing about the room and at the door when we're loving."

"Do I do that, kid?"

"All the time. You act like you're watching for something, like you're afraid of something coming in."

"That's a habit, kid. I can't help it. In jail I was always on the watch for the screws, and on the street I was always lookin' for bulls."

"There's nothing to be afraid of now, Benny."

"I know it, but it's a habit."

A habit of being afraid. . . . Lou was thoughtful. 'Poor boy. He must have gone through a lot. Terrible to be afraid so much that it becomes a habit.'

Benny knew that Lou was worried about him, and for a while he tried to banish her fears. He was cheerful, as he usually was, and he took care not to speak of junk or rackets for days at a time. He thought of them, though, and because he could think and not speak he began to resent it a bit. Lou shouldn't treat him like a baby. . . . But she was a good kid, and he would try to make her happy. He'd not worry her. She saw the change in him and became more at ease. She began to think that the demon had been exorcised.

And because catastrophe always comes when we feel most secure, she awoke one night and heard voices in the living room. Benny had a visitor, some one who talked in a low, droning voice that chilled her through and through. She got up and opened the bedroom door enough so that she could peer into the living room, and she saw Benny sitting on the edge of the table talking to a man who stood on the floor before him—and that man was Jew Murphy.

IV

HER first feeling was one of hopeless terror that left her unable to think clearly. She felt that she must sink to the floor, and her hand on the door-knob tightened spasmodically as she stared dumbly at the face of Jew Murphy. She had known instantly who the man was. Benny had told her enough of him for that. She recognized in him the symbol of all she had been fighting against. And now he was here in the flesh, fighting her in her own home. As her strength returned and the full realization of the menace rushed over her she felt an almost irresistible impulse to rush into the room and confront the man. She would go in and denounce Jew Murphy and all that he stood for. It was her right to fight for her love, to keep Benny from the one who would drag him back into the gutter. But for the moment she had not strength enough to carry out her half-formed purpose, and she had time to regain reason. She saw that she would gain nothing by openly declaring herself to Murphy. He would laugh at her, and she wouldn't know how to answer him. She wouldn't know just what to accuse him of. It would be better to listen first and learn what was afoot. She peered intently

through the narrow opening in the door and waited
for Jew Murphy to speak.

But it seemed that whatever had been the purpose
of his visit he was through explaining. She had
wakened too late to learn anything. He was picking
up his hat from a chair and turning toward the outer
door. As he reached it he turned and said:

"Just remember what I told you, Cokey. I know
what I'm talkin' about, see. You can't get away with
it, see."

"Take it easy, Murphy," Benny said. "I'm on
the up an' up with you."

"I know you ain't no louse, Cokey, see. I know
you're regular far's that goes. But you got funny
ideas, see. You let that moll make a chump outa
you, see."

"I ain't no chump, Murphy."

"Well, don't be one, see. Don't be a damn fool."

"I'm all right," said Benny. "I know my stuff."

"Well, the Big Fellow's got his eyes open, see.
He won't stand for no monkey business."

"I know it," Benny said.

"Well, it's good you do, see. You watch your
step. You're one o' the slickest little pushers in the
racket, an' there ain't no sense in you goin' haywire
over some dizzy broad. They're all alike. Women
don't mix well with rackets. They take all you got
an' queer the works. I'll see you at the joint. Take
it easy, see. I'm gonna screw."

He was gone, and Benny still sat on the edge of

the table, smoking a cigarette and smiling slightly. Lou stepped into the room and faced him.

"What's the matter, Benny?"

"Well, ain't this somethin'! When'd you wake up?"

"I heard you talking, Benny. Benny—what are you doing?"

"Smokin' a butt," Benny evaded.

"You know what I mean, Benny. What are you planning to do?"

"Nothin', Lou. Nothin' at all."

"What was Jew Murphy doing here, Benny?"

"Aw, he just came to talk over old times."

"Benny, why don't you tell me? Don't you trust me?"

"Well, what's wrong with *you?* You gonna start preachin'?"

"Benny!"

"Yeah, I know. Just the way you used to do. Always actin' like a little tin angel. What the hell's the idea anyway?"

"Please, Benny, don't talk that way."

"Well, I believe in sayin' what I think. No use talkin' nice. Nasty nice, that's what you are."

"I thought you loved me, Benny."

Benny looked at her with a peculiar, dreamy expression in his too-bright eyes. His face was pale, and she thought suddenly that he looked pitifully small and thin. She wished that she could get into his mind and understand why his lips seemed to

196

tremble a bit. There was, she knew, some sort of a struggle going on within him, something neither of them knew about. But he turned his face from her and laughed unnaturally.

"Love! What do you know about love? Do you think I fall for that old line? Love! That's funny."

"Benny, you know better than that. You know that nothing matters to me but our love."

"Love! I ain't a chump. I'm through."

She felt, deep within her, that this was just a phase, just a symptom of his disease, his drug-wrecked mind. She knew that all she had to do was have patience and he would soon get over it and be sorry for the things he was saying. There was nothing, she told herself, to grieve over, nothing to fear. They would go through many scenes such as this, but as time passed and the drugs were cleansed from his brain as well as his body, the scenes would come at longer intervals until there were no more. It was only a question of time until she would have him completely for herself. It was merely a matter of fighting off the drug, her rival. Drugs did not willingly loosen their hold on a victim. Long after the superficial cure was effected there was the hold on the mind. A dead habit had its ghosts. The ghost was speaking through the lips of Benny. Cokey Ben could not quickly die out of the body of Benny Wagner. She realized all this, and yet, because after all she was emotional and her nerves were strung to breaking tension, she broke down and quarreled with him.

"Benny, you're making a fool of yourself."

"Sure, I know. If I ain't a fool it ain't your fault. You tried to make me one. But I ain't a chump. You can't make a chump outta me. I was a damn fool when I quit the racket for you. I'm goin' back. I ain't a chump."

"Oh, chump, chump, chump! That's all I hear. You and your friends. Always talking about being chumps or making chumps of somebody else. You're so damned much afraid of being a chump that you can't see what's good for you. You make chumps of yourselves because you're so afraid somebody will make a chump of you that you won't let anybody do you any good. Damn them all is what I say. Ever since I came back you've been telling me about 'right guys' and 'chumps.' I can see through it if you can't. You're nearly thirty years old, and you act like a child. That damned Jew Murphy—"

"Jew Murphy is a good guy. He told me right. He says I been a fool to stick to you. Now I know it."

"Damn Jew Murphy! Damn him and all of his friends. You never had anything when you were with them. You stick to them and go to jail and rave about them being right guys. Who's this man they call the 'Big Fellow'? Do you know? Well, I do."

"Like hell you do."

"It's McTeague, the alderman. Hasn't he done
enough to you to wake you up? Oh, what's the use
talking to *you*? You can't see it. You can't see that
he killed your father and drove mine away from his
family and sent you to jail where you became a
junky, and even got his own son killed. You can't
see it—because he's a 'big shot.' A big pig is more
like it. A damned greasy pig wallowing in slime and
making himself fat off other poor fools who look up
to him."

"You don't know what you're talkin' about. Mc-
Teague ain't got nothin' to do with it."

"No, you're afraid to admit it. He's got you all
trained. He takes life easy while you and your
friends go to jail for him. Does he go to jail?
Damned right he doesn't. *You* go for him, and then
call him a 'right guy,' a 'big shot.' Chumps! You're
a fool, you and your kind."

"Aw, hell, shut up, woman. Shut up before I take
a soak at you."

"I know. You'd hit me. You and your love!
But you know I'm right. I told you ten years ago.
You used to rave about how that Chick McTeague
was a big shot. He'd get you by all right. I told
you then what a fool you were. Always following
the big shots. You can't see through them yet. All
your life you'll be a fool—a chump."

"You can't make a chump outta me."

"You damned little fool!   Will you never wake up?"

She shouldn't be quarreling this way—not with Benny. She seemed unable to control herself. She knew it, but something was driving her on. There had to be a release for all the fears and worries her mind had lately suffered. Now that she had broken loose she felt a great relief, as though she were casting a weight from her mind so that she might soar to the clouds. There was an exultation of the spirit that filled her with a sense of triumph even while she cried out in anguish for the love she seemed to be losing. Oh, it wasn't wise, for her to quarrel with Benny. He wasn't responsible for the things he said. It was the ghost within him talking. But perhaps she could drive the ghost away, make him realize his condition.

And then—what of her own frustration? All those years as the daughter of a barber who did not understand her, living amidst the sordidness of middle-class domestic strife, holding herself above the maelstrom of a degenerating community by the buoyancy of her hopes, her ambitions. Just now she had been swearing at Benny, cursing his associates. As they escaped her lips unbidden the words had rather shocked her. She realized then that environment will out, no matter how deep the gloss of training. She had trained herself, educated herself, but all the time she had lived among men who cursed and women who were careless, men who scoffed at decency and women who laughed with them. While her conscious mind had absorbed the culture and refinement she had longed for her subconscious had retained the taint of her sordid surroundings. That was why she could live with a man without marriage, why she found herself fighting for the love of a man who could never be anything but what he was. Her love for Benny had been the one concrete result of her subconscious surrender to past environment—her love for Benny and perhaps her infatuation for Carlo. But Carlo had been a part of her dream of success. He had been a stepping stone to fame as a singer. She had sacrificed something of herself on the altar of Art. Well, perhaps Carlo had been rather an unorthodox priest, but that had really been his part in her life. She hadn't loved him. Love for Carlo would have precluded any real love for Benny. She did love Benny. She would always love him. She had made him a part of her life. Her love for him had overshadowed her ambitions, her dreams of a career. She had been willing to give up everything just so she could make herself miserable with a little drug addict who was a neurotic. And Carlo had foreseen everything. He had told her that she would have her little hop-head but that she would never sing again nor be happy. Was there, then, no way of happiness with Benny?

"Love! You with your talk of love!" he sneered. "That was a good joke, wasn't it? We played a good game. Love! Well, that's all over now."

He was hysterical, she realized. She saw pain in his eyes. He was torturing himself. Some quirk in his nature made him try to destroy their love even though it was his most treasured possession. He loved her, and yet he denied that love and laughed at it. There was no mirth in his laugh. She was glad of that. She was glad that he didn't mean the things he said, even though perhaps he believed them himself when he said them. She was glad that while he said them he suffered. He did love her, and as long as he loved her she would fight for him. Well, she would play up to him, act her part. But it didn't seem like acting. She longed to take him in her arms and baby him, but she had to let him belittle their love because his mind was twisted.

And the thoughts in Benny's mind? What he thought seemed to have no bearing on the things he said. He wanted to cry, and he wanted to strike Lou and hear her cry out in pain, but at the same time he wanted her to love him. He wanted her to pet him and caress him, but if she tried it he would push her away. He didn't want her to touch him, didn't want to have anything to do with her, but he loved her and wanted to cuddle up against her and go to sleep. There she was with tears in her eyes. Well, she had no business butting in on his affairs, making him look foolish before Jew Murphy and the Big Fellow. She was making a chump of him, making him the laughing stock among the mobs. She didn't understand things. She said she loved him, but he was

suspicious of people who said they loved him. He
wanted to love her, but something was wrong with
him. There was something more he wanted, something she couldn't give him. And he couldn't love
her like she wanted to be loved. The junk had
taken some of the power to love away from him.
Junk was like a passionate woman; it left a man lifeless in a certain way. He was afraid of that. Afraid
she would turn from him when she found out. That
hurt him. She had no right to hurt him. She had
no right to make him feel inferior.

But he did love her. He wanted to love her. He
wanted to love her, but there was something that
wouldn't let him love her enough. There were
times when he felt sunk, times when he wanted to
break away and run wild. It was the junk, the longing for the junk. He didn't exactly have a yen now,
but there was an emptiness. Something was missing.
It drove him wild and made him want to hurt people.
It made him want to hurt himself. He could hurt
Lou, and when he saw her cry that hurt him. He
wanted to be hurt. God—if only he could go back
to the old schmeck and forget everything else. Well,
Jew Murphy—

Lou was crying. He looked at her, but said nothing. He lit another cigarette and went into the bedroom. Lou threw herself upon the couch in the
living room, her face buried in a pillow, sobbing.
He undressed and started to climb into bed. He
heard her sobbing, and he went to the door and said:

"Shut up that bawlin' or I'll give you something to bawl about."

She didn't answer. She tried to moderate her sobs, and he went back to the bedroom and got into bed. She lay on the couch, hoping that he would come to her. She waited. She wanted to go to bed, but she wanted him to come and ask her. She couldn't believe that he would be indifferent to her suffering. He would come and ask her to come to bed, and that would be the way they would make up. He wouldn't go to bed and leave her there alone on the couch. It would be sweet to feel his arms about her, to hear him telling her he loved her, that he was sorry he had hurt her. She waited. And after a while she heard his heavy breathing, and she knew that he had gone to sleep. For a long time she lay thinking, and she did not know of what she thought. She knew that she had waited, and the man she loved had been able to go to sleep while she suffered, and that somewhere, very soon, she must find a solution to her problem, else she would destroy herself.

V

SHE didn't sleep, and when morning at last came and she heard Benny stirring in the bedroom she made no move to leave the couch. She felt that she must wait, that he must make the first move. She hoped that Benny would feel sorry for her and come to caress her if she could just lay there until he could stand it no longer. She wanted him to want to make up. She wanted to show him that his treatment of her made a great deal of difference to her. If she should get up and go about the routine business of preparing breakfast he would feel that she didn't care so much, that she wasn't really hurt. She must make him know that his love meant everything, and that nothing could be the same as long as he turned from her. She just didn't dare get up and go about her household duties until he came to her and asked her to do so. And making up would be so sweet. She had thought of that often during the night. She had imagined how he would come to her in the morning and lean over her and kiss her and tell her how he loved her. At first she had thought that he would come before he slept, but after she knew he was sleeping she told herself that surely in the morning he would relent. His love for her would bring him to her. Never for a moment did she doubt that he loved her as much as ever.

But when Benny finally opened the door of the bedroom and came into the living room he said nothing. He must have known that she was waiting. She followed him with her eyes, silently pleading, but he ignored her. He even sang a little—that song about the cokeys' jubilee. On his face, though, she saw his suffering. He was torturing himself as well as Lou. He had deliberately hurt them both, and now he was throwing salt in their wounds.

He got his hat and she saw that he was going out. Now, if ever, she must speak, plead with him. She had waited for him to come to her, hoping that his love for her would not permit him to let her suffer too long, but since he had not spoken she must do something. Perhaps he, too, was waiting for the other to speak first.

"Benny," she said, "aren't you going to wait for breakfast?"

No answer.

"Benny, what is the matter? Why do you act this way?"

No answer.

"You're driving me insane, Benny. You know I love you."

No answer.

"I don't hold anything against you, Benny. I understand you. I know you don't mean the things you say. You don't know what you're doing."

206

"Oh, so you think I'm crazy, hunh?" he said bitterly.

"Not that, Benny. But I know how the junk affects people."

"Oh, yeah? Well, you know a lot, don't you?"

"Please, Benny, don't be this way."

"I ain't askin' you how I should act."

She went to him and tried to place her arms around his neck, but he thrust her away.

"Don't bother me," he said. "Leave me alone." His voice was lifeless, unemphasized. His face was averted, eyes half closed. He would not look at her.

"Benny, kiss me." She struggled to hold him.

"Don't bother me."

She tried to reach his lips with hers, but he drew his head back so that her lips barely brushed the tip of his nose. She tried to draw him to her and he tried to shake her off. She was desperate now, for she saw in his eyes that he was longing for her but that something was holding him from her. He wouldn't give in, and she knew that he could hold out forever against his own real desire to take her back. It was some twist in his mind that forced him to hurt her and himself, and she must fight for both of them. She grasped his arms and tried to force them around her. He wasn't strong enough to release her hands from his arms, but he could avoid her lips, holding himself rigid and distant. He was like a machine, cold and hard. The coldness and hardness must be overcome, and the futility of her position drove her to a new desperation.

"Kiss me, Benny. I know you love me, Benny. You can't make me think you don't. Benny, I *know* you do."

"Leave me alone or I'll hit you."

"I don't care, Benny. Hit me if you like, but after you hit me you'll tell me you're sorry. Go ahead and hit me."

"Leave me alone," he repeated. "I'm goin' out."

"Benny—don't go without kissing me good-by. You've *got* to kiss me."

He laughed a bit and tried to pull away. For a moment she stared at him unbelievingly, then she suddenly struck out with her doubled fist and caught him across the lips. A little spot of red appeared on his lower lip.

"You damned little fool," she cried. "I won't stand for it. I won't let you drive me insane this way. You're a stubborn fool. I could kill you."

She struck him again and again, and he stood with his arms at his sides, offering no resistance. As her passion subsided and she realized what she was doing she saw that a strange smile had parted his lips, and that he was looking at her expectantly. She knew, with a shock, that he wanted her to hurt him, that he enjoyed her outburst. There was blood on his lips, and she wanted to wipe it off, but before she could speak he smiled again and said:

"Well, ain't this somethin'!"

Before she could recover herself he had gone.

Well, was it all over? Had he gone for good, or was this merely another fantastic interlude of suspicion and mental flagellation that would end in mutual forgiveness and self-blame like the time when she had returned from New York and found him in jail? Perhaps this time he would be lost to her. What about Jew Murphy? Was that where Benny had gone now? Was the Irish Jew waiting for him, waiting to take him back into the underworld? Well—Benny had promised her to stay away from the stuff. If he broke his promise now that would mean he didn't love her. If he didn't love her she wouldn't have to—

'Why, what am I thinking? What am I thinking? I love Benny. I love him. I love him. I want him now. Oh, where is he. I love him. He won't use that stuff any more. Oh, I know he won't. If he does he won't love me. Oh, what is he doing? If he goes back to Jew Murphy he won't love me. He'll be breaking his promises. Promises . . . promises . . . promises. I promised him . . . if he breaks his promise I won't have to— Oh, no no no no. I love him I love him. Please, God, bring him back to me. Oh God make him love me always. Oh God, don't let him go back to them. Oh God, show me how to hold him. I love him, God, and You know what love is. Loving him makes everything right. Loving him gives me the right to do anything to hold him. Oh God, be good to us.

Be good to our love. Bring him back to me. Oh,
I'll kill myself. I'll shut all the doors and windows
and turn on the gas and lie down on the bed and shut
my eyes and go to sleep and never wake up and when
they find me they'll say I was a fool but I loved him
and couldn't live without his love and he will be
sorry and he will go back to his junk and try to forget me and some day he'll die too but we won't care
because long ago something died inside of us I
wanted to be a singer and get somewhere and I had
ability but now it's all gone and I can't do anything
but love Benny and that's all gone too maybe but I
can't sing any more and something died inside me
and I'm sinking down into something I'm afraid of
but I love Benny and I love Benny and I love Benny
and I can't be a singer like I dreamed I wonder if I
can recapture my lost ability something that was in
me a long time ago but something that has died and
left only a ghost but the ghost wants to come back
and there'll always be a ghost I wish I didn't have
an education and was not sensitive if I didn't have
an education and want better things I could be satisfied with Benny in the sort of life he belongs to and
we'd be happy because Benny should have a woman
who never had any dreams to give up because when
you have to give up dreams for love there is always
something gone something that has died sorrowfully
oh my dreams looked at me and sobbed when I
smothered them and they didn't quite die for a long
time not until I came back not when I was with Carlo

because Carlo understood and wanted to be part of the dream but he knew he would have to step aside when the dream came true but he understood and let me go and he knew what would happen Oh Carlo if I had loved you I could love you if Benny hadn't needed me if I hadn't promised Benny If I hadn't belonged to Benny if I hadn't had to keep my promises but a promise is sacred and it's binding on a person I must keep promises because I love Benny I love Benny I love Benny oh God don't let anything happen to our love don't let him go back to Jew Murphy and drugs don't let our love be hurt make him keep on loving me make him keep his promises don't let me doubt him doubt him doubt him I love him doubt him love him he loves me but don't let him do anything wrong don't let him get in trouble if he breaks his promises I won't have to— Oh, there I go—'

Why did that suggestion keep recurring? If he didn't keep his promises she wouldn't have to keep hers; that was what kept welling up in her thoughts. She couldn't clamp the thought down, it seemed. If Benny broke his promises she could break hers. The completion of the thought frightened her. She couldn't understand it. She loved Benny and wanted to hold him to his promises and wanted him to hold her to hers. Why then should this strange thought intrude itself? Well, she wouldn't try to understand it. She'd better not think about it at all. But why was she afraid to analyze the disturbing thought?

Why did she fear to know the meaning of that suggestion that should Benny break his promises she
wouldn't have to keep hers?   Didn't she want to
keep hers?   Didn't she want to stick to Benny?
Didn't she love him?   Wouldn't she hold on to him
no matter what happened?   Of course she would.
The strain she'd been under since yesterday had un-
balanced her for the time being.   She'd be all right
soon.   Yes, she'd be all right when Benny came back
and kissed her.

She went into the kitchen and prepared breakfast
for herself.   She must be calm and not become over-
wrought.   There was no need to go into hysterics
over a thing she knew would adjust itself.   Hadn't
he told her once before that she shouldn't mind him
when he had such spells?   Hadn't he admitted then
that he didn't know what he was doing sometimes.
She shouldn't worry about him at all.   She should
just wait until he outwore his abnormal mood and
came to himself.   He would be all right, she knew,
—but she couldn't help being afraid.   She couldn't
help appealing to him, fighting his moods that he
himself did not know how to fight off.   She knew
what she should do, how she should respond to his
actions, but she was too emotional to use her reason.
She had to let herself worry and grieve and fight
him.

'It's my own emotionalism,' she decided.   'I don't
use my reason when my emotions are upset.   If I
wasn't so emotional I might have been a great singer.

I've let emotions rule me, and my intellect has been defeated. Then, too, I'm afraid to ignore his actions. If I did that he might think I didn't care, and then I'd lose him.'

She was fighting to hold him because she belonged to him and he belonged to her. She could not lose a possession. There was a sense of security in knowing that some one had a claim on you, that there was some one to whom you had to account. And she still felt the maternal yearning for him that had made her long to fondle him when they were children together. How mature they had imagined themselves then! How they had prattled about eternal love and loyalty, and how she had dreamed of fame! Little Benny, the boy who was to be her very own through life; how she had yearned over him and loved him even then.

Sometimes, now, she wished that Benny had been larger, more of a man, so that she could feel more completely possessed by him. As it was, she always felt that she was his protector, that she must guard him. She had never felt that way about Carlo. No, Carlo had been the protector there. She had looked up to him and depended on him and his strength had been her strength. He was a man whom women loved because of his manhood. Benny was the type that could attract any woman because his appealingly boyish appearance awoke the instinct to mother and protect. But she loved him. She had always loved him, ever since she had known anything at all of love. And of course, no matter what he might do, she must keep her promises to him and she must always love him.

At noon she prepared luncheon, but he did not appear. This was the first time he had stayed away so long at a time. She tried to eat, but found that hunger of the heart had driven away appetite for food. She sat for two hours, utterly immobile, her eyes on her plate, seemingly detached from the room, from herself, from life. She was thinking, but her thoughts were unconnected ramblings of the sub-conscious through the conscious mind, and got no-where. At last she roused herself with a start and cleared the table and washed the dishes.

He came in at seven o'clock and ate dinner silently. She knew that he was watching her, and that he was smiling ever so slightly to himself. He did not speak to her after dinner. While she washed the dishes and cleaned the little kitchen she heard him singing to himself. She recognized the tune as it seeped faintly through the closed kitchen door, and she listened to catch the words. He had a clear, un-trained tenor voice, and when he used it on senti-mental ballads it was strangely effective. He was singing an old popular song:

> "I'm sorry, dear, so sorry, dear,
> I'm sorry I made you cry.
> Can't you forget, can't you forgive?
> Don't let us say good-by.

214

One little word, one little smile,
One little kiss, won't you try?
It breaks my heart to hear you sigh—
I'm sorry I made you cry."

Was he singing it to her? She felt that he was, but she didn't dare go in to him and answer the question in the song. Benny must be grieving for her, she thought. He was singing his sorrow, his plea for forgiveness. He, too, was very emotional and sentimental. She remembered the times when he had cried over her, when he had been entirely unashamed of his tears. That time in the jail when they had kissed through the mesh of the screen; again when he told her about her letters he had refused to read and the ones he had read and cried over. He was such a child, such a baby. He wanted to be loved and petted, and he could cry because he had hurt her. He was crying now, crying in that song. She could hear the tears dripping from the words.

Yes, he was a child, a baby, but he was an animal child sometimes. She might go in there and try to take him in her arms and he might turn and snarl at her. Perhaps he wouldn't be able yet to give in.

At nine o'clock she went to bed. Benny, in the living room, was singing again, and he had gotten out an old, unfinished bag he had started to make with beads in jail. He sat in the room and worked on the bag just as he had sat during those long nights

215

in jail, and as he worked he sang the songs he had learned in jail. Lou, in the bedroom, felt the burning moisture gathering in her eyes. Poor kid, he was living over again now his nights in prison. He was unhappy, singing his heart out because he loved her and yet couldn't love her. She wanted to go to him, wanted him to call her.

And now he was singing another song, another old one that had been popular just after the war. His voice was very tender as he sang:

> "I'm glad that I can make you cry,
> I'm glad that I can make you blue."

She listened until the end, and thought that she understood when he finished:

> "It proves that you love me when you sigh—
> I'm glad I can make you cry."

For a time he was silent, working carefully at the bag, never missing a bead. His fingers moved swiftly. Only occasionally did his eyes stray to her bedroom door, and then back to his work or perhaps to the outer door. His eyes were nervous as always, but he did not stop working. Once or twice he smiled palely, a sad little smile that curled up one corner of his lips as though in satiric scorn of himself. He was thinking:

'I'm a damn fool I guess . . . a chump . . . a fool. . . . I'll never get anywhere . . . she's a good kid. . . . I don't wanta hurt her. . . . Oh, I

want her to know I love her . . . but she can't make
a chump outta me . . . she's all right . . . she's a
good kid . . . she's been good to me . . . I gotta
be right with her . . . I won't be a chump though.'
Then he started to sing again:

"In the land of beginning again
Where broken dreams come true,
Though we've made mistakes, that's true,
Let's forget the past and start life anew.
Though we've wandered by a river of tears
Where sunshine can't come through
Let's find that paradise where sorrow can't live
And learn the teaching of forget and forgive
In the land of beginning again
Where broken dreams come true."

Broken dreams! She knew that he had issued the
invitation in words more expressive of his real feelings than any he could have originated himself. She
should go out to him now, take him into her arms
and go with him to the land of beginning again.
Why didn't she have the courage to go out and face
him? Why must she let this chance slip by? Perhaps by morning he would be out of the mood for
reconciliation. But she had better wait. He had
not really committed himself yet. She knew that he
was capable of laughing at her if she took his singing
literally. He meant the songs all right, but after
all he had not spoken really. He had conveyed his
meaning with reservations. He might be too stubborn, too proud, to admit his feelings openly.

But after he had been silent awhile she could bear the suspense no longer, and she called out:

"Benny—"

A second of silence, during which she sensed that he had suspended his work expectantly, then—

"Well, what d'ya want?"

"Are you coming to bed?"

"Yeah," he answered slowly, "sure I am. I'm goin' to bed right away."

She relaxed in relief, and in a moment she heard him burst out with that gay, ridiculous junky song:

"If I was a millionair an' had lots o' coin
I'd buy a big plantation, I'd raise heroin;
Piedmonts an' Meccas I'd have growin' on trees.
In a house built of M where I could jab at ease,
I'd have forty thousand layouts all inlaid with pearl
So each hop-head that I know could bring along his girl
An' each chump with a habit would come leapin' like a
     rabbit
Down to that Cokeys' Jubilee."

He must be all right now. He was back in his old gay, carefree mood. She waited. Suddenly she sat up in bed and listened fearfully. It was the sound of the squeaking springs on the couch in the living room. And as she listened she saw the streak of light under the door suddenly vanish. He had gone to bed on the couch.

Well, she must do something now. She had waited a day and a night for him, and now she was facing another night. She couldn't go through with it. She'd have to go to him now.

When she touched him on the couch he turned over and laughed a little and told her to go away and not bother him. She took his arm and shook him. She had left the bedroom door open, and the light from the bedroom made his face faintly visible. She could see that again he was struggling with himself. She tried to draw him to her but he pulled away.

"Don't bother me," he said. "Go 'way."

"I will bother you," she cried. "I'll bother you plenty."

She jerked the covers from him and tried to pull him from the couch. He hung on. She struck him across the face, then began to beat his chest with her fists. She knew that she was hurting him, and yet he was smiling, almost laughing. She struck him a heavy blow on his side and he doubled up in pain, unable to catch his breath for a moment. When he could speak he said:

"Well, ain't this somethin'!" He was laughing at her. She bent down and tried to kiss him. He placed his hand over his lips. She jerked it away and struck his mouth again. He laughed quietly. She was furious.

"It's not fair for you to treat me like this," she said bitterly. "I can't stand it any longer. I'll be a nervous wreck. You've got to get over it."

"Don't bother me."

"You act crazy. What is the matter with you anyway?"

"Nothin's the matter with *me.*"

"Well, what have I done that you should treat me this way?"

"Aw, why don't you quit?"

"You act crazy. You act like you're all charged up with dope."

"Naw, I ain't charged up. Don't bother me."

Suddenly she was very quiet, sitting on the floor beside the couch. A great fear was clutching at her heart. A suggestion had taken root in her mind and like a magic flower of evil it had sprung instantly into full bloom as a certainty. Charged up! He must be—he *was*—using junk again. Jew Murphy —mornings and afternoons away from home and away from her—peculiar looks—his fear of her gaze —all the significant little facts piled themselves up in her mind as fertilizer for the growing certainty that Benny had gone back to his habit. She could only sit and brood dumbly over it. He seemed to sense the tenseness in the atmosphere, and he stirred uneasily. Finally he reached over and took her hand.

"What's the matter, kid?" he asked.

"Oh, Benny—everything is the matter. You know it—you know it."

"Don't cry, kid."

"I won't. No, Benny, I won't cry much in a

minute—soon as I control myself. But—Benny—
I'm going to—know the truth about you."

"It's all right, kid."

"Good God, it's not all right!"

"Don't get excited."

"I'm going to go after that damned Jew."

"What's he got to do with it?"

"Benny—I know all about it."

"Well, let's go to bed."

He left the couch and they went to the bedroom.

"I'm sorry, kid," he told her when they were in
bed. "Guess I must be a bug."

"You're just a fool," she said. "But I love you
anyway, and I'm going to do something."

"What you goin' to do, kid?"

"I'm going to cure you—again."

"Aw, I ain't usin' it, Lou."

"You are, Benny. I should have known it before.
You broke your promise, Benny."

"Well, I ain't used much. I didn't mean to break
my promise, Lou."

"You forgot our love, Benny."

"No, I didn't, Lou. Never. Gee, I musta been
a bug. Gee, kid, I hate to see you cry like you did
last night. It hurt me. I wanted to love you. I
wasn't asleep all night. I fooled you. I made you
think I was asleep. But I cried, kid, honest I did.
But I know you love me. After the way you acted
last night no matter what ever happens you can't
ever say you didn't love me."

"I'll never want to say that, Benny. But you nearly drove me crazy last night. Don't ever do it again."

"I won't, kid. I don't know what was the matter with me. Didn't you hear me singin' to you to-night?"

"I didn't know whether you meant it or not," she said.

"Of course I meant it. Gee, Lou, I always mean it."

"I hope so, Benny."

"I guess I was worried. Jew Murphy's been on my tail. Wants me to start pushin' again. He's been after me a month. An' he's goin' with Ethel now too."

"Ethel?" Lou suddenly became all attention.

"Sure. Ethel an' the old lady are back in the old house again. Been back a week."

"I thought they sold out and moved to New York."

"They just sold the saloon. Ethel dragged the old lady off to New York to spend the money they got from my old man. I guess they spent about all of it all right. They got a boarder stayin' with 'em now. Some guy came from New York with 'em. Big shot I guess. Come here to do business with some bootleggers. Knows McTeague too. Jew Murphy says he owns a big joint in New York. Night Club. Joint called the Cheese Carlo."

"The Chez Carlo!" she couldn't help exclaiming.

"You know it?"

"Yes, Benny. Didn't I tell you I worked there?"

"Maybe you did. I guess I don't remember."

"And Carlo is staying with your stepmother?"

"Carlo? Oh—emh-humh—that's it, is it? That's the gee's name?"

"They call him Carlo," Lou said.

She was aware that he was regarding her suspiciously in the dark. She had betrayed too much interest in the name of Carlo. She should be more careful. And then, realizingly, she thought:

'But I'm as guilty as Benny! He was keeping something back from me, and I found it out. Now I'm keeping something from him. Will he find it out? I should have told him. It's going to be hard. It's going to be very hard.'

"Benny," she began, taking a sudden plunge, "do you love me enough to forget about the past?"

"Of course I do, kid. I love you enough for anything."

"If there were other men, Benny?"

"I don't care what you did before you came to me, Lou. I've got you now, an' that's all I want. I wasn't no angel an' now I'm on the junk again."

"Well, Benny, there *was* a man. I went to him when I thought everything was all over for us. When I learned the truth about you I left him in a minute and came to you."

'I didn't know I loved Benny then,' she thought. 'Benny had dropped out of my life, and I didn't know I loved him so I went to Carlo. Why—it was funny! Why didn't I know I loved Benny when he wasn't near me? How was it possible for me to put him out of my mind when I thought he had forgotten me? I let him go so easily after the first heartbreak was over. I cried and was despondent for a while, but it didn't take me long to accept the new condition. I never thought of that before.'

"I don't care," said Benny. "It wasn't your fault. Anyway, you're here now an' you won't ever have another man."

"No, Benny, not ever—another man."

"We'll always love each other, hunh, kid?"

"Of course, Benny. But while I was gone were there any other girls? Regular girls, I mean—not just women of a night."

"No. Not even for a night, kid. Why, Lou, I was on the junk all the time after I got outa jail that first time. I was on the junk—and you know what that means. When a gee's got a heavy habit he just ain't got no use for girls, Lou. He just can't use 'em, that's all."

'Oh, my God,' she thought. 'Oh, my God.' She couldn't speak. She lay staring up toward the ceiling in the dark. Soon she knew that Benny was sleeping wearily in her arms, but she could not sleep. She was thinking of this thing she had now to fight, and of Jew Murphy and how she could cope with him. Sleep fled farther and farther from her as she grew more and more furious at Jew Murphy. And Alderman McTeague. Fat, corrupted, smirking Alderman McTeague, the man who had first caused Benny to stay in jail long enough to become a drug addict. Jew Murphy was working for him. Jew Murphy was trying to get Benny to work for him. Jew Murphy had given Benny another habit, trying to enslave him again.

She must fight. She must save Benny so that their love should survive. She had given up everything for that love, and now that love must not be killed by drugs.

"No use for girls," he had said. "Just can't use 'em." What was to be the ending? She had heard of women who became addicts just to hold the men they loved. They had used the stuff so that they might have something in common with their lovers. If a man couldn't love a woman because he was using drugs, then the woman would become a junky too so she wouldn't care about his inability to give her the love she wanted. They'd have the companionship of drugs if not of sex.

'Maybe I'll end that way,' she thought with a shudder.

But what about Carlo? He was here, had been here in the city a week, and yet he hadn't been to see her.

'But of course he wouldn't come,' she reasoned. 'He knows I am with Benny. Knows I love Benny. Knows there can't be anything between us again. He wouldn't come here.'

Well, to-morrow she would start her fight. There would be some way to win out. She would discover some way to beat the thing that was trying to lure Benny away from her.

'Carlo . . . Carlo . . . Carlo.' The name recurred persistently in her thoughts, running through her mind in a peculiar sort of rhythm. 'Carlo . . . Carlo . . . Carlo . . .' Carlo meant something here in the city. She wanted to see him again, and yet she felt that she could not. She had to fight this thing that stood between her and Benny, and if she was to fight effectively she must throw aside all thoughts of others. She must not think of Carlo. And yet—she was facing the biggest problem of her life, and she could not help feeling vaguely that somehow the answer lay in Carlo. . . .

VI

ALDERMAN McTEAGUE sat behind his shiny mahogany desk in his gaudy office, smoking a rich black cigar and talking to a young, eager-faced man who wrote swiftly on a pad which he rested on his knee. When McTeague felt the urge to publicity he merely had to send out a call and a reporter came on the run. McTeague's newspaper appearances acted as a smoke screen for his undercover activities. Speakers for the Anti-Saloon League, the Anti-Narcotic League, and the W.C.T.U. often quoted the obliging alderman enthusiastically. He had letters from all the anti-liquor organizations thanking him for his generous financial aid. McTeague knew his benefactors. Prohibition had made him rich and a power in local politics, and he intended to do all in his power to keep the wets from victory. Every time he gave a check to the cause of Prohibition he raised the price of bootleg or Scotch for a few days to make up for it.

He looked at the young reporter and blew a cloud of heavy smoke around his head before he said:

"Got everything down okay now?"

"Yes," said the reporter.

"Read it off. Let's see how it sounds."

The reporter read: " ' "Any man who uses his eyes, and has the ordinary intelligence to understand what he sees, will realize the value of Prohibition from the economic standpoint," said Mr. Mc-Teague.' "

"Better change that to 'Alderman McTeague,' " the politician interrupted. The reporter sighed and made the change, then read on: " ' "As I look from my office window I see concrete proof of this new prosperity. Directly across the street is a bank, built on the site of an old saloon. In the old days of easy booze there was not enough money in the district to support a bank. Now I am told that the new bank depends almost entirely upon the people of this neighborhood for its existence. The truth is that men who once spent their hard-earned money in the saloons are now saving it for their children." ' "

"That's okay," McTeague approved. "Sure, that's just right. Working men are saltin' their money away in the banks now."

He did not think it pertinent to add that he himself had two million dollars in that bank, nor that the two million had been made by the illegal traffic in booze and narcotics. Nor did he mention the four millions he had in other banks, distributed about the country for greater security in case anything should go wrong. Had he disclosed the fact that bootleggers' rings had deposited ten million dollars in that one bank in one year the reporter's story might have been different.

"Yeah," McTeague encouraged, "that's all right. Let's hear some more."

The reporter continued:

" ' "Ten years ago," said Alderman McTeague, "there were six saloons in the block in which my office is now located. They were rowdy places, filled nightly with men who had better been home with their wives and children. I remember them well, for I have been inside them. But Prohibition has changed all that. Where one of the saloons stood in all its corruption a high class restaurant now stands and flourishes. Men who drank themselves unconscious in the old place now go there to eat nourishing food. The restaurant manager buys supplies from the local dealers. Every one profits. Prosperity smiles upon those who once had to struggle for a living." ' "

"That's not bad," said McTeague. He thought it best not to add that the name of the prosperous restaurant was the "Silver Tassel" and that he owned it and used it as a blind for bootlegging and narcotic distributing industries. He did not lie when he said it was a prosperous place. Under the management of Jew Murphy it certainly had been highly profitable. Years ago it had been August Wagner's saloon.

" ' "All along the street," ' " the reporter continued reading, " ' "can be seen new places of business. There are hotels, barber shops, restaurants, shops of all kinds. They came here because under

229

Prohibition the men of the district had money with which to buy the necessities of life—money that formerly had been spent in the saloons." ' "

As he listened to that, McTeague chuckled quietly to himself. 'Yeah,' he thought, 'there's plenty of new places all right. There's the Palace Hotel. Nice girls and plenty of good booze for the cash customers. There's Mike's Chili Parlor. See what the boys in the back room will have! And there's the Bon Ton Café. Good lookin' place in front, with white-topped tables and everything. I hear Joe had three new card tables put in upstairs last week. An' he's a good customer for the Alki too. Those card-players sure like their booze. I better tip Captain Bain off to those new tables. He'll have to squawk for a bigger cut. The more he clips 'em for, the more I get—an' I want all that's comin' to me, you bet!'

The reporter read the rest of the "interview" and departed. When the writer had gone McTeague opened the door to an inner office and went in to where Jew Murphy had been waiting for him.

"All right," McTeague growled, "I'll talk to *you* now."

Jew Murphy had looked up startled as McTeague entered. Now he rose hastily to his feet and tried to smile ingratiatingly.

"Sit down," roared McTeague. "I've got plenty to say to you."

230

Jew Murphy almost fell into the chair and looked up at McTeague expectantly.

"What was the slip-up on that shipment from Havre?"

"Aw, Boss, that couldn't be helped. You know how it happened. The papers was full of it."

"Well, something must have gone wrong with your organization."

"No, Boss. The mistake was made by those saps on the other side. The shipment landed here all right, and was bonded in the warehouse to be shipped on to Frisco and then to Shanghai. That part was all right. The inspectors wouldn't have opened anything, because stuff that's just goin' through this country on its way to another country ain't opened when it's bonded while it's here. But those damn fools over there had marked the shipment as *Chinese dolls*. Some wise inspector just wondered why Chinese dolls should be shipped to China where they make 'em, an' he investigated. My organization was all right. My men was all ready to steal the stuff from the cars before they reached Frisco, but of course they never got the chance."

"Well, something's got to be done, that's all. You've got to get some more stuff somewhere quick. We're losin' money. There was two hundred grand worth lost in that shipment. And we're short of stuff now. There'll be a panic. It's up to you to get out and hustle before the junkies start hollering."

"Prices have already gone up," said Jew Murphy. "We had to boost 'em."

"Get out and do something," McTeague shouted. "What do I pay you for?"

"All right, Boss. But what can I do?"

"You've got to round up a good mob and send 'em out on a prowl, that's what. You've got to do it before a panic is on."

"Well, I can do that all right, Boss. Got any suggestions?"

"Do I have to tell you everything? There's a big stock in the warehouse of the National Drug Supply Company. There's *plenty* there. You know what to do."

"Take it over?"

"Don't ask questions. I'm not telling you to do anything. You use your head and straighten things out, that's all. Get out and work."

"All right, Boss."

"And have you got that Benny Wagner back?"

"He's comin', Boss," Murphy grinned. "He's back on the stuff."

"Good! He's a wise boy in the racket. You never have done much good since you lost him. Damn that woman!"

"Yeah, Cokey Ben was good because he didn't care what he did, see? He was wild. I could use him an' then drop him till I needed him again, an' he never beefed. He's the best pusher in the racket, and he keeps his mouth shut."

"Well, get him to do the dirty work on the National Drug Supply job. He'll pull it all right."

"All right, Boss."

"Be sure you have a good alibi. Be at the Silver Tassel all night when it's pulled off. I don't want you to get pulled in for anything big. Don't ever let 'em get anything on you."

"They never have, Boss."

"I know it. But don't ever let 'em. If you do, you're through."

"I'll let Cokey Ben pull the job. If they get him he won't talk. He's a right kid all right."

"Well, even if he talks they can't drag *me* into it," said McTeague.

"No, Boss. You're safe. Why, even I couldn't prove nothin' on you if I ever wanted to talk."

"You better not ever want to talk."

"I know better, Boss. I know you can't be touched. Hell, if anybody rumbled the cops about you they'd just laugh. You own 'em!"

"Well, that's enough. Go on and get busy with Cokey Ben."

"I got to be careful, Boss. That broad of his would be wild if she found out. She made him promise to lay off."

"Well, don't let her get in the way. You need Cokey, and you got to get him in spite of her. Good pushers are hard to find. If we want to make the heavy sugar we got to have good pushers. We can't let a woman interfere."

233

"All right," said Murphy. "I'll bring him around. If he gets sore at her he'll do anything I tell him to. He's easy when he ain't with that broad."

"Go and get him," said McTeague. "And get busy quick. There won't be another big shipment from the other side for six weeks yet, and in a week from now the panic will be on."

"In a week from now we can send out the word that the pig is fat," Murphy amended confidently. "Just watch me do my stuff."

When Jew Murphy had gone Alderman Mc-Teague went to a cabinet and poured himself a generous drink of brandy, after which he smiled contentedly and lit another expensive cigar from which he did not remove the band. He sat behind his desk and looked out the window. The sun, sinking behind his own building, shone in the glass of a window across the street and reflected back into his eyes so that he squinted and looked down, but the reflection also shone on the cluster of diamonds in his immense platinum ring and sent out a flash that seemed alive, and he found that this flash did not hurt his eyes and he did not have to squint.

VII

I T was late afternoon when Lou came to her deci-
sion. Yes, Carlo must be the answer to the
problem. She would go to him, knowing that whatever he might think he would at least understand,
would not condemn her, would help her as he could.
Perhaps they could take Benny away with them
someplace and force him to take a cure. She and
Carlo could hold him, perhaps make him captive in
a room, tie him to a bed, keep him from the drug,
keep him from Jew Murphy and others who profited
by his habit. She and Carlo. . . . Was Carlo, then,
to be definitely tied up with her? She had been
thinking of Carlo in strangely intimate terms. She
had been thinking of him as her co-protector of
Benny. Why, she had been thinking of Benny's
relation to her and Carlo in terms of a child to his
parents!

But that idea of tying Benny up to a bed was too
melodramatic. Like a dime novel or a cheap movie.
People didn't do those things in real life. Or did
they? She tried to remember all the things she had
heard, all the cases Benny himself had told her of.
Yes, there had been such cases. There was the
woman who had tied up her man for two weeks, until

he became quiet and purged, she thought, of the habit. And then she had let him up, and he had murdered her. Benny would never do anything like that, of course. Benny loved her too much. Anyway, perhaps the story wasn't true. Perhaps it was part of his imagination, something that had happened in that shadow realm of his poisoned mind.

No, she couldn't carry out anything quite so preposterous. She would have to plan carefully, patiently, subtly. She would have to strike at the causes, not the results. She would have to reach Jew Murphy, through him reach the men higher up, reach Alderman McTeague.

But was there any top to this mountain of systematized vice? Who was the man above McTeague, the man even higher and the men higher and higher? Even the law couldn't reach them. They got the little cogs in the vast machine, but the big wheels still ran smoothly because the oil was poured on by invisible mechanics, and spare parts were ever available. She had learned that just by listening to Benny in his more confidential moments.

But McTeague was the head of things in this district. She was sure of that. Why, everybody must know it. How could they help but know it? Didn't *she* know it? But of course she could know things not revealed to ordinary people. She had become a part of the underworld, was let in on its secrets. But, after all, what *did* she know? What could she prove on McTeague? What, for that matter, could she

prove on Jew Murphy? She knew that he was the
cause of Benny's ruin, but what was her word against
the combined strength of his backers, his protectors?
What could she do to fight something that had the
protection of the police? A police captain was receiving graft from a hundred vice establishments,
was receiving twenty-five thousand dollars a year
from one booze and narcotic ring. Benny had told
her that, and Benny knew. Under this captain were
six lieutenants who had to follow their captain or be
hounded from the force, and they were getting their
share of the swag, so that they really didn't object
to doing what Captain Bain told them to do. And
the sergeants followed the lieutenants, and the
policemen followed the sergeants—and how could
she hope to do anything against the man who paid
the captain in the first place?

Oh, but there must be a way. Carlo must know
something to do. Carlo would know how to
straighten everything out so that she could feel secure once more and be happy with her Benny. They
would help Benny in spite of himself, in spite of
everything, in spite, even, of the big shots who controlled the underworld and forced the little fellows
to do their dirty work for them. It was the little
fellow like Benny who took the chances, went to jail,
often went broke and even hungry, because he
thought he was on the inside of a good racket.
Hundreds of Bennys, thousands of Bennys, maybe
millions of Bennys for all she knew, went out every

day and every night and sold drugs on the streets,
or transported truck-loads of booze overland from
the landing points to the inland cities, or held up
drug-stores, or stuck up men on the streets, or black-
mailed merchants—just because the big shots like
Al Capone or Alderman McTeague needed more
money to swell their inflated egos. All those poor
deluded Bennys were composited in her Benny Wagner, and she must save him. She and Carlo must
save him. She and Carlo. Carlo. . . .

Get to McTeague and the work would be done.
Get to McTeague. How? Well, there was always
some way to do anything if only the way could be
discovered. McTeague sat aloof, looking with
greedy, cruel eyes at the treasures his worshipers
laid at his feet. He was the god of the underworld.
He was the Big Shot. He made money and had
power and he was a big shot. He was a god to be
worshiped by all the Bennys who saw him through
magnifying glasses.

'He's a fat pig,' she thought. 'A fat pig.'

She remembered that expression used by the drug
traffickers when they wanted to pass along the good
news that there was plenty of dope on the market.
'The pig is fat! Yes, that's him all right. A fat
pig. He's been swilling and wallowing in crime so
long that it's made him fat, just like all pigs get
when they have some one to feed them all they want.
The pig is fat. The pig is fat, but, oh, how lean are
those who feed him! Why don't they do like the

farmers do? If they feed a pig and make it fat, and
then find they haven't anything for themselves to eat
—why, they eat the pig of course. If they could only
eat the pig, eat the pig, eat the pig. He wouldn't
be in the way any more. But the pig tells them to
go on feeding him, and if they feed him enough
there'll be something left over, and they can gather
it up and feed themselves.'

But such thoughts wouldn't get her anywhere.
What she needed now was action. She'd have to
start something at once, or Benny would be lost
beyond redemption.

'Maybe I'm a fool,' she thought suddenly.
'Maybe I'm a fool to try to save him. He might
drag me down.'

But no. Carlo would help. They'd have Carlo
to see that nothing happened to them. Carlo would
know what to do. Try as she would to picture her
future alone with Benny she could not exclude the
thought of Carlo always being with them, always
helping her with Benny. Benny was such a
child. . . .

She hurried over to Benny's old home, where
Angela Chester and her daughter now had a boarder
who would help her. Ethel wasn't at home, and
Angela became timidly flustered when Lou appeared
at her door and asked for Carlo. Ethel had warned
her mother about this very possibility, had told her
not to spread the news that Carlo was there. Ethel
wanted him for herself, was vain enough, arrogant

enough, to imagine that she had a chance. But Angela, without Ethel there to reënforce her, hesitantly admitted that Carlo was in his room.

"Well," said Lou impatiently, "call him."

"I—I'll tell him," Angela quavered.

Lou stood in the hallway and tapped her foot nervously on the floor while she waited for Carlo. When he appeared, descending the stairs, she saw that Angela was directly behind him, an anxious, almost pleading look in her eyes. Angela was utterly afraid of Ethel, of what she would say when she heard of this meeting.

"Get your hat, Carlo, and we'll go somewhere to talk," Lou said evenly.

He looked at her penetratingly and smiled. She tried to smile, but something caused her lips to vibrate, draw down at the corners, tremble. She blinked her eyes, steadied her lips, waited for him to get his hat. When he returned she was smiling a sculptured smile that did not touch her eyes.

"You can talk in the parlor if you want to," Angela timidly suggested. "Nobody will bother you."

They ignored the unseen worm in their path, left her standing in the hallway feeling crushed. Out on the sidewalk Carlo took Lou's arm and said:

"Baby, I've been waiting for you. I knew you would come."

"You sent no word, Carlo."

"No, Lou; I didn't need to. I knew you'd hear

about me. I knew you'd look me up if you needed
me."

"I do need you, Carlo. That's what I wanted to
talk about."

"I knew you'd need me, Lou. That's why I came
here with the Chester women. It's funny, baby, but
that Ethel thinks I came to be with her. She's going
out with a bum named Jew Murphy to make me
jealous!"

"Carlo, you've got to help me. It's about Benny."

"Oh, your little hop-head. I remember. You
love him."

"He's driving me insane, Carlo. It's this Jew
Murphy. He's got him using heroin again."

"Yes, I know. I hear things because I'm in with
the big shots, you know. I have to do business with
them."

"Well, I must stop him, Carlo. You'll have to
help me."

"What can we do?"

"We can take him away from Jew Murphy.
Maybe we could lock him up."

"In jail?"

"Oh, no! In a room where we can cure him."

"And so you think you can do it, baby? Do you
think you can stand to see him suffer?"

"It's the only way I can think of, Carlo."

"Then we must do it, Lou."

"When he comes to himself he'll be glad I did it.
He loves me."

"He ought to love you. If he doesn't love you he must be sick."

"Sick? Oh, Carlo, it's worse than sick. That stuff takes him completely out of himself. He wants to make me happy, but he can't do anything but think of the stuff he uses. It works on his mind. He gets to worrying about his failure to love me as he should, and suddenly he goes all to pieces and won't speak to me for hours—or days."

"Yes, Lou, I know. And he thinks you're trying to put something over on him. That's the way they do. I have seen them. My wife was one."

"And that was why you left her?"

"That was why I left her. I could not cure her, and I would not sacrifice my future for a woman who could not give me what I had the right to expect from a wife."

"But I'm going to cure Benny. I'm going to make him love me like—like a man."

"Like I could love you, Lou?"

"Carlo!"

"I'll always remember some things."

"It's best, sometimes, to forget."

"It's impossible, sometimes, to forget."

"Why can't you forget?"

"You left so much of yourself with me. You could not go away and remove everything. I kept so much, Lou. I kept the thought of your sacrifice when you gave up your singing to come back to your little hop-head. That gave me the memory of a

242

great love and I always wished that it could have been mine. To know that you loved him like that, that you could love any one like that, filled me up with something that cannot be taken away. And you left a song, Lou."

"A song?"

"Just a little song that you sang for your little hop-head when you thought you had lost him. When you had gone, I thought to myself, 'She sang this little song for the little hop-head when he was lost to her, but now she is going back to him she won't need it any more. I'll keep it for myself.' And so, Lou, I've been singing your song, 'I'll Still Be Your Pal If You Need Me,' all these months."

"If it hadn't been for Benny—"

"I know, baby. If it hadn't been for Benny you would have loved me. But doesn't that mean that you did love me? When one loves truly there is never any 'if' about it. If you had truly loved Benny you never could have seen me at all—even as a second choice."

"Carlo, sometimes I've half wished that there had been no Benny. I've given up so much for him, and he's made me so miserable. But I can't help it, Carlo. I've been very close to Benny since we were children."

"Yes, Lou, but you never can get really close to a junky."

"He wasn't always one, Carlo."

"He'll always be one."

"No, Carlo; I must cure him."

"And if you cure him, and then find that still he can't love you with passion—what will you do?"

"I'll keep on trying, Carlo. You see, he really wants to love me. He feels badly about it. He loves me with his whole being, but when he realizes that there is nothing to back up that love, nothing of what a normal man gives a normal woman, he is heartbroken. Carlo, I've seen him cry over it."

"But he goes back to the stuff, even when you are with him."

"His will is weak."

"It will never be stronger, Lou."

"Mine will have to be strong enough for both of us."

"I wish you would come back with me, Lou. We can be married. My wife got a divorce at last."

"Ah—then you are free?"

"No, Lou."

"Not free?"

"No, Lou; I am your slave."

"Carlo, there's no use. I can't leave Benny."

"But he is leaving you."

"It's the drugs. I can't forget how sweet he used to be, how we loved each other and were happy before I went to New York, before he first got in trouble. Because of that I must keep him."

"If you wanted to preserve a piece of fruit you would do it before it became spoiled. You wouldn't take the rotten, moldy fruit and try to save it because once it had been sweet. You would throw it away, wouldn't you, Lou?"

"Of course."

"Well, that is what I did with my wife. That is the only thing you can do with Benny if you want to be happy. You cannot preserve the spoiled fruit."

"And now you think I should throw it away?"

"Rotten fruit in the same dish with good fruit spoils everything, baby."

"I love him."

"That is the answer to a great deal of unhappiness."

"I can't help it, Carlo."

"Some day you will wake up."

"As long as he loves me and needs me I shall never leave him."

"Does he love you, Lou? Are you sure?"

"I can see it in his eyes even when he is in one of his terrible moods."

"You have funny ideas sometimes. I think you'll wake up. I don't think you love him at all. You just feel loyal to him."

"Carlo, you're full of surprises. I like to talk to you. There are times with Benny when I starve for conversation."

"The little hop-head does not talk well? I know. I have experienced it. Nothing but lies, lies, lies."

"Not lies, Carlo. He believes what he tells. But he has certainly told me some outlandish tales about his adventures."

245

"And he tells you he loves you?"

"You mean that he may imagine that too? Well, what does it matter? If he believes it, it's true. Whatever one believes is true to the one who believes it, Carlo."

"You've built up a strong wall about your love, haven't you, baby? You've thought it all out. That shows you've had your doubts. You don't really love him."

"I do, Carlo. I do."

"Well, then, we'll see. We'll see if we can help him."

"Come over to dinner to-morrow night, Carlo. I'll have him meet you. Then we can do something."

"Yes, baby, we can do something."

"And, Carlo—can't we get McTeague some way?"

"McTeague?"

"Yes, Carlo. He's the head of all this business. If we can get him we can stop a lot of it."

"You've learned a lot, haven't you, Lou? And how can we get him?"

"Don't you know enough about him? Can't you tell what you know and put him in jail?"

"I know all about him. I know enough to know that I can't put him in jail, even if I wanted to. No, Lou, they never arrest the big fellows. The big fellows wouldn't be big if they didn't know how to keep out of jail."

"Isn't there any way?"

"No, baby. If we started anything we'd go to jail before he would."

"Carlo, where is it all going to end?"

"Must it end?"

"We're all so helpless. Benny. We must see him dragged down with thousands of others just because a great criminal is too big to put in jail."

"Lou, the only way to put an end to it is to make all the little chumps who work for him see how he's taking them in, make them desert him. If all the big shots were exposed as the cowardly egoists they really are, the little fellows all would desert them in disgust, and the underworld would be overthrown over night."

"And that can't be done? No, I see it can't."

"What we need is the laugh cure. Make all the big shots like Al Capone look foolish, make the underworlds laugh at them, and see what happens."

"It sounds interesting—the laugh cure."

"Yes; show them how their heroes are brave because they go on the streets with armed body-guards, because they do their fighting with machine guns, or by proxy, because they are protected at every turn. Brave? Not one in a hundred has the guts to stand up and fight man to man. McTeague is so fat he waddles. Jew Murphy would faint if any one walked up and challenged him to a fight when none of his friends were around. They're afraid to do

247

their own stealing even, so they hire chumps to do it for them. To me it's all a big joke. I'm tired of seeing them in my night-club."

"Why don't you sell out, Carlo."

"Maybe I will. I've been thinking of something."

"A new business? What is it, Carlo?"

"I won't tell you now. I'm going to wait until I see how we come out with your little hop-head. But, Lou, I want you to go out with me Friday night. A concert. Cortez is playing the violin, and Mazsonzinni is singing."

"Carlo! I'd love it."

"Then I will see you to-morrow night. Go on back to your little hop-head now, and I will go back to the house where Ethel will want to know what you said to me."

"But you won't tell her?"

"I'll tell her to go to hell, baby."

And as they separated and he turned back in the direction of his temporary home, he was thinking to himself: 'She's coming back to me, the little singer. She's coming back to me after all. After to-morrow night she will come back to me. After the concert she will decide.'

VIII

BENNY sat silent while Jew Murphy told him how he could help to flood the city with a deluge of drugs to take the place of the supply that had been confiscated by the police. Plenty for himself, too, he would have. Plenty of schmeck to keep himself charged for a long time. He could keep enough here in the apartment to feed his habit for months. Jew Murphy was very careful to emphasize all that. Benny would not have to worry about his stuff. Just think of it! All he wanted, to use as he liked.

Benny saw paradise opening before him, saw a haze of ineffable happiness enfolding him, felt himself floating down the stream of dreams to forgetfulness. And then—what of Lou? If she could drift with him— But she would be left behind, stranded, unable to enjoy the things he could not live without. Jew Murphy had talked softly, insinuatingly, injecting the idea of happiness with junk into his mind subtly, slowly, invitingly. He had spoken words like needles full of heroin, words to bring memories, dreams, desires. But nothing of Lou. Benny tried to resist, did not want to resist, thought he had better resist, did resist weakly:

"I guess I better not do it."

The softness left the voice of the Irish Jew, menace crept in, menace etched with greed.

"You better," he said. "Yeah, Cokey, you better."

"No," said Benny, stronger in his second assertion, "I can't do it."

"You know what happens if you don't?" The creeping menace leapt out now from the voice, revealed itself, became brave and dared to threaten openly. "If you don't come in on this you don't get any more junk, see?"

"Oh, yeah?" Benny's voice rose into the room, then weakened and broke and trembled between them. His eyes suddenly darted up to meet those of Murphy, and then he sighed softly and let his eyes rove around to the door. The silence surged with fear until it swelled out and burst into a cry:

"I got to have my H, Jew. You know I got to have it."

"The word'll go down the line that Cokey Ben is off the list."

"I can get it," said Cokey Ben weakly.

"Not in this town, you can't get it, see? You'd like a bang right now, wouldn't you, Cokey? Well, you can't have it, see? I got it right here in my pocket, but you can't have it. You can't ever have it."

"I don't need it right now, Jew."

"No? Well, you will. Yeah, you will, Cokey.

To-morrow you will. Day after to-morrow you will. Think of it."

Benny did think of it. A minute ago he hadn't needed the stuff much, but now that Jew Murphy had made him think of what would happen when he couldn't get it, he began to want it more than anything. He wanted a shot now, just to convince himself that he could get it.

"Hell, Jew, give me a break, will you? I promised Lou——"

"Yeah—you promised Lou. Fine piece o' work she is."

"Lou's all right. She's been good to me, Jew."

"You're a chump, see?"

"No, I ain't, Jew. I never been a chump."

Benny knew how he could knock a man cold just with a sudden lift of his knee. He never stood for monkey business from the gees. He didn't care how much he hurt them. He would use his knee, and he wouldn't care even if he ruined the gee for life, made him useless. But he couldn't do that to Jew Murphy. Jew Murphy was a big shot, the god of the underworld, and you had to let a big shot say anything he wanted to and do anything he wanted to do. Only another big shot could do anything to a big shot. The only time you could hurt a big shot, unless you were crazy, was when another big shot paid you to do it. If any of the mob had talked against Lou he would have shown what a tough gee he was, but from Jew Murphy he had to take it.

"She's been makin' a chump outta you, see?   I know," Murphy insisted.

"She's all right. She's a square kid."

"She's a two-timin' broad."

"No, Jew. She ain't."

"I can prove it, see?"

"You tryin' to give me the needles?"

"No. She was livin' with a guy in New York, see?"

"She was workin' at a night-club."

"She was livin' with the guy, Cokey."

"She loves me, so how could she do that?"

"I know the guy. He's boardin' with your old lady."

"Boardin'—say, you mean that gee Carlo?"

"Yeah, that's it."

Benny was thoughtful, doubtful, fearful, hurt; Cokey Ben was suspicious, jealous, did not doubt that she had made a chump of him. He'd been a fool to take her back those other times. She'd made him think she loved him, was true to him, had always loved him. He had let her pull the wool over his eyes. He had listened to her, let her love him and make a fool of him. Well, this was the end. He wouldn't be a chump.

"Okay, Jew; I'm with you," he said.

"That's the way to talk, Cokey. The mob is waitin' for you. I told you just what to do. You tell them what they need to know, see? Don't let any of 'em get away with any of the stuff, see? You

252

put it all where I told you, an' it'll be taken care of, see? You can take your share an' keep it, see?"

"I got it all right, Jew. Yeah, I understand everything."

"This is Thursday. You pull the job to-morrow night."

"Sure, Jew, I'll do it."

"Now we'll celebrate, hunh?"

"Sure, Jew, let's get charged."

Jew Murphy fixed up a shot of hot water for himself, making Cokey Ben think he was taking a bang of H. But Cokey Ben didn't care what Jew Murphy took as long as he gave *him* the real McCoy. He started to sing:

> "If I was a millionair and had lots o' coin,
> I'd buy a plantation, I'd raise heroin——"

But Murphy interrupted the song with the needle, and Benny was ready with arm bared. Murphy took his arm and smiled:

"Here, Cokey, let me give you the jiboff. To hell with women when we got the old schmeck, hunh, kid?"

"*Good* old schmeck!"

"Hold out your arm."

"Mmmmmm! That's the money, Jew. The real McCoy."

"Have a smoke."

"Sure, Jew. Wish it was black stuff 'stead of tobacco."

"No, Cokey. You gotta keep lively. Bang up with plenty H."

"Maybe a snootful o' coke Friday night, hunh?"

"Sure, that's the idea. Give you plenty moxie."

"I got a lot of moxie anyway, Jew."

"I know you have, Cokey."

"I ain't afraid of nothin'."

"Sure, I know it. That's why I let you in on the big jobs, see?"

"You're a good guy, Jew."

"Where's that broad?"

"Out somewhere."

"Well, why don't you pack up an' move out while she's gone? No use stickin' to a no-good broad. Get away before she turns you up to the bulls."

"She wouldn't do that."

"She might, Cokey. She ain't no good."

"The dizzy bum! I been a fool all right. What if she'd put the finger on me?"

"That's what she would a done all right."

"Well, ain't that somethin'! I been a chump!"

"Broads get a guy goofy sometimes."

"She had me in a fog, Jew."

"Well, have another smoke."

"Sure."

They smoked another cigarette, and then Jew Murphy gave Benny another shot of heroin and Benny went to the bedroom and packed up a suit-caseful of his clothing. When he came back into the living room he took an old envelope and wrote

a short note on the back of it. He left the note on
the table and picked up the suit-case.

"You got everything?" Murphy asked.

"Yeah, I guess so."

"Well, let's get goin'."

Just as they started out the door Cokey Ben remembered something. He went back into the bedroom, opened a dresser drawer, took out a small stack
of bills, put them in his pocket, smiled to himself,
went out and joined Jew Murphy.

"I guess I wasn't such a chump after all," he said.
"I clipped her for her roll."

"That's the way to treat 'em," said Jew Murphy.

Lou sensed the emptiness of the apartment as soon
as she opened the door. In an instant she saw the
note on the table, and like an explosion the truth
flashed through her mind. She walked slowly over
to the table, picked up the envelope with the peculiar
back-handed writing that was Benny's style, read it:

"Go back to that guy you lived with. I'm through.
The best of chumps wake up some time."

The best of chumps! Through! The guy you
lived with! He must have heard about Carlo. But
she had told him there had been another man, had
asked him how he felt about it, had been told that he
didn't care about her past as long as he had her now.
Where had he gone? She went into the bedroom
and saw that he had taken his things. Through . . .

255

so he said. Was it just another spell? She'd have
to wait. He'd come back, come back and tell her
he'd been crazy.

A dresser drawer was open. She went over to
close it, saw that the money was gone. Gone. The
remainder of Carlo's five thousand dollars. Over
two thousand dollars. Gone. He had taken it. If
he could do that he must have gone for good. He
had never done anything like that before, never tried
to harm her. Now he had stolen from her. The
full sense of what had happened swept over her, and
for a moment she stood swaying, letting the hope
drain slowly out of her heart. The room was
smothered in heavy futility, so that there could be
no movement, no coherent thought, for a little while.

After a while she went into the kitchen and made
herself an omelette and a cup of coffee, and then she
went to bed. She was very much alone, but somehow she didn't seem to mind so much after a while.
Maybe he meant what he said, maybe he was really
through with her for good, but she wasn't going to
cry about it this time. After all, she had some rights
to happiness even if he didn't believe in her. Perhaps this was for the best, perhaps it would be best
for him not to come back. She'd just wait, now,
calmly and philosophically. She wouldn't wear herself out with tears and worries. If he came back in
the morning, begging forgiveness, she wouldn't re-
ject him. But she wasn't going out looking for him.
She was going to show him that he could push her

just so far, and then she'd stop fighting for him.
Yes, she had been fighting for him too, not merely
for herself. He had needed her to bring him back.
He had wanted to love her, and he had needed her
to force him to do what he really wanted to do. But
she wouldn't fight for him any more, not after what
he had done this time. The theft of the money had
decided her. Every time she thought of that open
dresser drawer, the disarranged contents, the missing
bills, she felt anger creeping over her and urging her
to revolt. She had never felt angry with Benny
before. Stealing from her had been such a despic-
able trick, so utterly dishonorable.

And that note. "The best of chumps wake up
some time." It sounded so definite, so final. Written out in visible letters the words seemed more real
than they ever had sounded coming from his lips.
His lips just made transient sounds that vibrated for
a quivering moment and fell silent, devoid of sub-
stance, but there on the back of an old envelope was
something convincingly tangible, his words brought
to life where she could see them and touch them.
She pictured the letters, leaning over backward, some
of them bending a little in the middle like old men
slipping on the ice. She imagined Benny's thin little
hand sliding over the paper with a pencil that left
cutting words that would stay behind after he had
gone. Had he smiled as he wrote? Had he
laughed? Or had he hesitated a moment while
memories brought tears to his eyes? She knew that

his real feelings wouldn't have made any difference. He had turned from her before while his heart was yearning for her. But the words written on the old envelope meant something this time. They were written and would not become silent. They stayed before her eyes, and became notes for the queer music that writhed through the rhythm of her thoughts.

Well, now, that it was all over she could go to sleep. Now that she had made up her mind not to cry again she could quiet her nerves and rest. To-morrow night, at dinner, she would show the note to Carlo. He would know what to do. Maybe he would think of some way to get McTeague and Jew Murphy. Maybe they could go out and find Benny. Anyway, they would go to the concert and hear great music. Cortez, the newest sensation among violin-ists, would play. And Mazsonzinni would sing. She, too, was a soprano. She had once thought it possible that something lay ahead for her. Perhaps she shouldn't let memories or those old dreams dis-turb her now. Best to let wounded, helpless, hope-less ambitions die. Well, to-morrow night—Carlo— They would talk of—Benny. . . . They would talk of Benny . . . Benny. . . . It was good to sleep now.

IX

NOW that she knew there was no use to worry, no use in letting Benny's erratic ways get the best of her, she felt at peace with a strange contentment. She was no longer angry, no longer in a turmoil within. She was only a little sad, feeling that things had borne down too heavily on her, had crushed her beyond struggle. She would not weep now, for tears no longer came unbidden. It was best to accept things as they came, to live from moment to moment, passively. And yet she felt the need to overcome the system that supported Jew Murphy and Alderman McTeague. It was hopeless, though, she realized. Only an organized revolution in the underworld could dethrone the despots. Either that or an awakening of the public, a revolt of the voters. The sense of her smallness engulfed her. When she thought about it the injustice of it appalled her. She could suffer and cry out for surcease, but what did the suffering of the little people matter when millions of dollars clamored at the doors of the politicians? How could the little people be led to liberation when they worshiped their exploiters? The gods of the underworld were the Big Shots, and woe to any who should dare to take the names of the gods in vain. Benny, suffering and helpless in their grasp, would yet fight for them and go to prison for them —even die for them. Well, what was the use in grieving over him and ruining her own life? She would go about her life calmly, without tears.

She could not, of course, be cheerful. One is not gay when one is suddenly stranded on a desert isle. That, she told herself, was exactly her situation. She had broken loose from the past, and it had drifted away from her, leaving her cast up on a little desert island of the present. The tide was rising, and there was peril on all sides. From her island of jeopardy she could not see the shore of the future, whether it was rock-bound and sinister or a smooth beach lapped by a gentle bay. To save herself she must find a means of passage across the raging sea of the underworld that surrounded her. Perhaps the sea would suddenly wash over her little island and destroy her. It didn't matter, now. When one has made up one's mind to face the worst, there need be no fear, no vain hopes.

When Carlo came to dinner he looked at the table, set for two, and smiled queerly.

"The little hop-head is not here?" he asked.

She showed him the note, and for a little while neither of them said anything. The words of the note spoke between them at the table, and filled them with silence. Finally she made a little nervous gesture with her hand and said:

"You see, now, what I have been going through?"

"I know, Lou. It is finished, then—the affair with the little hop-head?"

"He may come back," she said with a sagging weariness. "He always has, Carlo."

"You mustn't always be waiting for him to come back. He goes, and he comes, and he doesn't realize what it means. He is supported by the stuff he uses, and he always does what he wants to do. He always knows that he is coming back. On his part there is no anxiety. It is not fair to you. You stay and wait, and you do not know."

"I'm not going to worry any more. I'm past that now. I'll just wait and get along as I can."

"You're wrong, Lou. You'd better get away while you can."

Perhaps, she thought, this was her chance to escape from her island. Carlo would be her means of passage.

"But he depends on me, Carlo."

"Sooner or later, if you stick with him you'll be just like him—a junky."

"Oh, no!"

But she had thought of that very possibility, hadn't she? She had remembered women who had become addicts because of their men.

"You will," he said. "No woman can stand it. What would you be doing to-night if I hadn't been here?"

"I don't know."

"No, Lou—you don't know. But the other day

261

when you came to me you were pretty far gone. What if you hadn't had me to go to? Baby, you'd have broken all up."

"I haven't thought of that."

"No, I know you haven't. But you do see now, don't you? You've got to break away. There is no use in staying here where you can't be happy."

"But how do I know I'd be happy if I went away? Oh, Carlo, I don't know what to do."

"There is your singing, Lou. You could go very far. You have real talent. You proved it at my club."

"That's all past now."

"No, Lou. I have a plan for you. Come with me. We'll be married. I'll sell out the night-club. I said the other day that I was tired of this business. I am disillusioned, Lou. I want peace. I want to get away from the bootleggers and crooked politicians. They made the night-clubs, baby. To run a night-club you have to admit them to your life. In the old days a café was a respectable business with decent entertainment and good liquor, but that is over. The night-clubs are run by the underworld, and I am tired."

"But, Carlo, what will you do?"

"I'll take you to Europe. You can go there and study. You can be a great singer."

"Oh, Carlo, I can't decide. I can't."

"Think about it, Lou. Think about yourself as a star at the Metropolitan."

262

"The way I used to think ten years ago," she mused. "Carlo, I can't decide now. I'm not sure I can leave Benny."

"It's up to you, baby." He looked at his watch. "We'd better hurry," he told her. "The concert is ready to start."

Half an hour later, as they drove to the theater, she wondered if she could make up her mind to set sail from her desert island.

X

A SLENDER, pale-faced, esthetic-looking young man came out into a white spot-light and lifted a violin to his sensitive chin. The man was not impressive, for his body was small and anemic and without attraction. But when he lifted the bow with his slender fingers and drew it gently across the taut strings of the violin the audience forgot the man and clung breathlessly to the soaring notes. This was Cortez, the great Cortez who was a sensation wherever music was loved. He had come here to play to-night with Mazsonzinni, the great coloratura, Mazsonzinni who could enthrall an audience with her every whisper.

Lou and Carlo sat in the balcony, no other seats having been available when Carlo sought to purchase them the day before. But when the first sobbing sigh arose from the vibrant violin in the hands of Cortez Lou was glad to be there, glad to be in the balcony, would have been glad to be in the topmost gallery to hear this ecstasy of tone. The throbbing notes floated over her, filled the vast auditorium, quivered in the air, beat against the walls, beat against her soul, pleaded with her mind, rose again to heights of tragedy, calmed into the poignant beauty of heartbreak, hung suspended for a moment on a note of deeper grief, then, weighted with tears, fell through the atmosphere, breaking up into the final little cascade of running arpeggios, settled in the hearts of the listeners, in the heart of Lou.

Cortez was bowing, and the spell was suddenly broken by the outbreak of applause. Cortez assumed entity as a man again, an unprepossessing little man who bowed for something his violin had done.

Lou touched Carlo's arm and whispered:

"It was wonderful, Carlo. His feeling for—for *motif*—Carlo, he makes you understand what is in his heart—he carries you away."

"I knew you would like it, Lou. One of Cortez' own works."

"I know," said Lou softly. " 'Bereavement,' isn't it?"

"That is the one. You have kept up with your music?"

"I had to, Carlo. I had to read about all the new things in music."

"It was becoming a romantic memory to you, wasn't it? You loved it, and you thought you never could have it again."

"I couldn't quite forget it," she admitted.

"You were still dreaming. You still dreamed of your music. I know."

"No, Carlo. I didn't let myself think of it in that way. I just tried to be satisfied in knowing what others were doing in music."

265

The orchestra began the introduction to Mazson-zinni's first number.

"Ah, now we shall hear her."

"Rigoletto," whispered Lou.

"Yes, Lou; 'Caro Nome.'"

"I love it."

The diva appeared, bowed regally with the applause, smiled tolerantly at the orchestra leader, and began the aria. Lou sat entranced. As the famous voice reached out and embraced her she felt drawn to the stage, saw herself there in the place of the star, heard her own voice rising on the crest of the highest notes. When it was over she sighed with a little sob-like catch in her breath, then sat silent while the audience applauded. She did not applaud. There were things too great for mere handclapping. She had just heard a voice such as her own might have been had she gone on as once she had planned. First, the sobbing grief of the violin had softened her, made her sympathetic, and now the singer had taken advantage of her mood, had made her want to sing, to achieve the ultimate glory of her dreams. Perhaps there was a tinge of envy in her reaction, envy lightly engraved with resentment that another great singer should so easily win the acclaim she felt that she herself might have deserved. Her ambition once more was aflame.

"It was great, wasn't it?" Carlo whispered.

"Oh, Carlo—if *I* could do it."

"You can, Lou."

"I feel that I can," she murmured dreamily.

"You shall have your chance," he promised.

And so, for another hour, Cortez and Mazson-zinni alternated in their attacks on her emotions, their appeals to her love of music, their invitations to her ambition, their urge to her instinct for competition. Between selections Carlo did his part in directing her thoughts toward the justification of her own talents. He felt that this night would decide her, that this dramatic demonstration of the things she might have would win her to his plans. Since his appeals to her reason had failed he had taken this means to appeal strongly to her emotions. He believed, hoped, that he was winning.

Back in her apartment they sat down to hot chocolate and buttered toast.

"Lou," he said, "you have a better voice than Mazsonzinni."

"No, Carlo. Don't tease me."

"You have, Lou. I should like to hear you sing that Mad Scene from Lucia after she sang it to-night. You would put into it more passion."

"She was superb, Carlo."

"Yes, Lou—but she is too heavy. She sings with restraint, like a duchess who is afraid of her dignity. You, if you sang the Mad Scene, would know that it should be with abandon, with feeling—with madness."

"Carlo, she sang it perfectly."

"Not as you could sing it."

"You should be a director, Carlo."

"I have wanted to, Lou."

"You?"

"You are surprised, but it's true. I could really do it—with you for inspiration."

"Carlo, you certainly are one surprise after another."

"Come with me and we'll both be artists."

"Carlo, I think I'll do—"

Suddenly the door burst open, slammed shut. They faced it, startled.

"Benny!" cried Lou.

He was standing by the door, panting for breath, looking wildly excited, clutching an automatic in his hand.

"Benny—what are you doing?" Lou cried. She and Carlo had sprung from their chairs, stood by the table, facing the disheveled Benny. He gasped in surprise on his own account, then laughed a little shortly.

"Well, ain't this somethin'!" he exclaimed. "What you doin' anyway?"

"What is the matter, Benny? What are you doing with that gun?" She stared at the automatic fascinatedly.

He seemed suddenly to remember something. An expression of fear crossed his face, then he made a dash for the bedroom.

"I gotta hide," he explained. "I gotta hide before the bulls crash in."

"The bulls—"

"Hide me, you damn fool." An' lock that door. The bulls are comin'."

"Benny—"

"Damn it, woman. Somethin' went wrong. The bulls got wise to the job to-night. They're comin'. Can't you snap out of it?"

"That gun, Benny—"

"T'hell with that. I gotta fight 'em off, don't I?"

"Benny! My God, Benny—"

"Oh, shut up. You gotta hide me some place an' stall 'em off. If they dig me up I'll start smokin' 'em with the gat, that's all."

"Benny—you're full of cocaine. What have you done?"

"Don't ask questions. We tried to stick up a joint an' we got a rumble, that's all. One o' the gees plugged a cop in the leg."

"Benny—and you came here to bring them in on *me?*"

"Where else would I come? You love me, don't you?"

"After what you did—"

"Oh, forget it. You love me, so help me out." For the first time he seemed to notice Carlo. "Who's this guy?" he demanded.

"Lou," Carlo said, "I think we'd better get out of here."

"Oh," said Benny. "I guess this is Carlo, hunh? Well, you better beat it. Screw, before I get tough."

"Benny—"

"I'll smoke him sure." Benny swung the gun menacingly.

Lou walked calmly over to Benny and took the gun from his hand.

"Don't be such a fool," she said. "You aren't safe with a gun."

"You mean this guy ain't safe when I got a gat," Benny corrected her. "What you think you're gonna do about it, hunh?"

"I think I ought to beat you up," said Lou.

Benny looked at her in puzzled amazement, slowly blinking his eyes. Lou, standing so calmly there, telling him she'd like to beat him up, taking him lightly, refusing to take seriously his most dire threats, suddenly reminded him of the Lou he'd known as a child. She'd always treated him, then, as a child. Well, she couldn't start that again now. He was too old for that stuff now.

"You better send this guy away," he said ominously. "You belong to me."

"Benny, do you think you had the right to come here?"

"You said you loved me, didn't you?"

"I do, Benny."

"Then you'll help me."

"Lou, think of yourself," Carlo broke in.

For a moment the three stood silent, two forces drawing the third in a strange mental tug-of-war. This, Carlo knew, was the crisis. She would decide now for all time, either to stay with Benny or to go with him and accept happiness.

Lou was miserable. She knew what she should do. She should renounce Benny and go to Carlo, but on the other hand—didn't she owe something to Benny? Could she desert him now when he was in trouble? But would he have come back to her if he had not been in trouble? The words of the note came back to her in a flash, vividly as though she held the paper in her hands before her eyes. "The best of chumps wake up sometime." Was that his real belief? And the money. That had hurt. He had stolen from her, had not cared how she might get along without funds.

'You promised to love him always, to trust him always,' said the voice in the back of her mind.

'He doesn't really love me,' she argued. And then—there was the music. Mazsonzinni sweeping a vast audience with her miraculous voice. That could not die out of her, the memory of that voice, the feeling that she, too, could sing greatly.

For a moment that hung heavy with suspense she hesitated, then she walked over and touched Carlo's face with her hand.

"We'd better go, Carlo," she said.

Benny slumped a bit, took on the puzzled expression he had worn so often in childhood when he had gone off alone to cry the hurt from his heart.

"You goin' with him?" he asked in a small voice.

"Yes, Benny."

"You leavin' me?"

"You left me, Benny. You came back only because you were in trouble. I'll go and leave you
here. I won't drive *you* out."

"Well, ain't this somethin'!" He seemed suddenly lost, as though reality had dropped from
around him.

"I can't stand it any longer, Benny."

"Well, ain't this somethin'!" he repeated, totally
unable to think of anything else to say.

"Good-by, Benny."

She went over and kissed him, and then she and
Carlo started toward the door.

"Wait a minute," Benny called. "You don't need
to lam. I guess I got excited. Got the bull horrors.
They're tailin' me all right, but I got time. I can
hide out in a good place. I just wasn't thinkin' when
I come here. Lou, I guess I was thinkin' of you, an'
I was runnin' right into a trap here. 'Course this
would be the first place they'd look for me. I musta
been a bug to come here. I guess I just couldn't
help comin' to you, Lou. I'll go now, an' you don't
need to worry. Don't cry about me. I'll be all
right. I was a bug to try to keep you, kid. You
made me happy for a while, an', Lou—whatever happens now you can't ever say you didn't really love
me. I know you did. Good-by."

"Be careful, Benny," Lou warned, trying to keep
back the tears. This parting was not so easy, even
with Carlo there to support her. It was so fraught

with finality. She knew, now, that he was definitely passing from her life. She had loved him so much, still loved him so much. Suddenly she was sobbing, and Carlo was trying to soothe her. Benny opened the door and went out into the hall. As he closed the door he called softly:

"Take it easy, kid. It's all for the best I know."

He was gone, gone forever . . . forever.

"Don't cry, Lou," said Carlo.

"I loved him," she sobbed.

"It's hard, I know."

"Did you see—the look—on his—face when—he went out?"

"His heart was breaking, but it will mend."

"He thinks—I've been making a—chump—of him."

"No, Lou. He realizes his condition when he thinks."

"I've hurt him, Carlo."

"He hurt you."

"Oh, Carlo, let's get away as soon as we can. I want to forget everything. Staying here reminds me of so much."

"Do you love me, Lou?"

"I love you, Carlo. I don't know how it is, but I love you and I still love Benny—but I want to marry you."

"I know, Lou. I know what you want."

He took her in his arms, and pretty soon she stopped crying.

273

XI

COKEY BEN sat on the end of his cot in his cell and talked to Jack, the former trusty at the County Jail who now had a job as "runner" at the state prison. Cokey Ben was doing time now, his first bit in the "Big House." He hadn't got away with the loot that night in the city, so nobody had come to the front for him. That hurt him a little, but he understood that the big shots couldn't risk exposing themselves just to help him. Of course, if he'd been successful and had got away with plenty of junk from the drug ware-house he might have expected the bosses to hire a lawyer for him and pull political strings. But Cokey had been a failure that night. One of the mob had been too free with his gat, and a cop had got his leg smashed. Somebody had to do time for it, so they let Cokey take the rap. Those things would happen. He did think, sometimes, that Jew Murphy might at least send him a buck now and then to buy tobacco. But Jew Murphy was wise. He probably knew what he was doing. He was a big shot, and Cokey knew better than to doubt his wisdom.

"Say, Jack," said Cokey, "did I ever tell you about

the time I saved a flock o' cows fer my old man when he run a big ranch in Texas?"

"No, Cokey. Did your old man have a ranch in Texas?"

"Sure he did, Jack. My old man's been in a lot o' places."

"Yeah, I guess he has all right. But what about the cows?"

"What about 'em? Whatchu mean?"

"The flock o' cows. You said you saved 'em."

"Oh, yeah. You butted in an' made me get mixed up. Don't butt in when I got somethin' to say. Ain't I told you that before?"

"I'll dummy up," said Jack.

"Well, the old man had a big flock o' cows out in the fields, an' them cows was gettin' skinny as jail-birds. The old man couldn't figure it out at all. Said there wasn't no reason for cows to get skinny when there was plenty o' nice dry grass for 'em to eat all over the place. Why, Jack, them cows was so skinny they rattled. Yeah, they rattled their ribs together."

Cokey paused to light a cigarette, offered one to Jack, lit both of them, continued:

"Well, I got to thinkin' 'bout them crazy cows. I went out an' watched 'em, an' damn if I didn't find out they wasn't eatin' none at all. No, sir, them cows wasn't touchin' all that nice dry grass what was just like good hay. 'Well, ain't this somethin'!' I says, an' watched some more. Funny thing about it was, I seen cows on other ranches all around us eatin' an' gettin' fat. Why the hell couldn't them cows o' ours eat like other cows? Was they too ritzy to eat offa the ground? Well, I tried to figure out what it was all about, an' I went an' asked a few questions.

" 'What kinda cows is them there damn fools?' I asks the old man. 'They're Jersey cows,' he says. So I thinks some an' I gets an idea. I been in New Jersey, an' I know somethin' 'bout how the grass looks there in the summer. It's nice an' green. Sure it is. Well, this Texas grass was all dried an' browned by the hot sun an' no water. No wonder Jersey cows wouldn't touch it! They was used to green grass. They didn't know what the brown stuff was, an' they was starvin' to death."

"Well," said Jack, "how did you save 'em?"

"There you go buttin' in. You always got somethin' to say."

"Sorry, Cokey. Please tell me how you saved them cows."

"Well," said Benny, "if you'll keep still I'll tell you." His cigarette had gone out, and he stopped talking a moment to strike a match on the sole of his shoe and relight it. He took two long drags from the cigarette and then went on:

"I seen somethin' had got to be done if them cows wasn't gonna kick the bucket, so I went over to San Antonio an' bought five thousand pairs of green glasses. I took 'em back to the ranch an' put 'em on the cows, an' you oughta seen 'em go for that grass then! It looked green through them green glasses. In a month all them cows was fat enough for market. The old man was sure glad. He had all his dough tied up in them cows."

"Gosh," exclaimed Jack. "Five thousand cows in green glasses! That musta been some sight."

"It was," Cokey agreed. "Yeah, it was kinda funny. The cows got so's they used to come past the house every morning to get their glasses on 'em. They'd file past the porch an' I'd put the glasses on 'em, then they'd bark at me to say thanks an' go off to eat."

"What happened to all them cows?" Jack wanted to know.

"They died," said Benny. "They got killed. A big bull killed 'em."

"What for?"

"Well, one day this bull was out eatin' grass with all the cows when his glasses fell off. He looked around an' didn't see no grass that was green, an' he seen the cows eatin' anyway. Guess he thought they was all crazy eatin' the brown dirt that way, so he just stands lookin' at 'em kinda puzzled for a while, then he starts nosin' into 'em. He tried to push 'em away, but they wanted to eat, so he got mad an' started hornin' 'em with his big horns, an' killin' 'em. Pretty soon the poor cows was so excited tryin' to get outta his way that they started fallin' down an' steppin' on each other. They was in a panic. When it

277

was all over we went out an' found a bunch o' dead cows. The old man took 'em over to Mexico an' sold 'em to the greasers to make chili con carne."

"Say," said Jack when he had digested the tale of the cows, "whatever became of that broad you was hangin' out with?"

"Oh, her? Say, she was a dizzy piece o' work, all right. I chased her out, Jack."

"Good fer you. Women ain't no good anyway."

"Right. I'm done with 'em."

"They get you in jams."

"Sure, an' then laugh at you."

That night, Cokey Ben sat in his cell making a beaded bag. As he worked he sang:

> "If I was a millionair and had lots of coin,
> I'd buy a big plantation, I'd raise heroin—"

When somebody yelled at him to shut up he laughed and sang louder, but after he got into bed he got to thinking about something and he buried his head under the blanket and sobbed bitterly.

'God,' he said to himself, 'why the hell couldn't *she* be a junky? We'd a been happy then. Oh, well, who cares? To hell with it all. Women ain't nothin'.' But he sobbed himself to sleep.

THE END

278

www.ingramcontent.com/pod-product-compliance
Lightning Source LLC
Chambersburg PA
CBHW031003260626
47169CB00002B/683